## About the Author

John has been a nurse, a tutor, a lecturer, a manager and a counsellor. He is married to Betty and between them they have six children and nine grandchildren. This is John's first published book, with a further book of short stories waiting in the wings.

# Dedication

This book is dedicated to Trevor Robinson who coaxed, cajoled and challenged me to write something.

I am not sure what this is but it is definitely something.

Thanks Trevor.

Trevor Robinson
1st August 1945 – 14th November 2014

John Orr

# TALES FROM A QUIET MAN

AUSTIN MACAULEY
PUBLISHERS LTD.

A CIP catalogue record for this title is available from the British Library.

ISBN (Paperback) 9781784557713
ISBN (Hardback) 9781784557720

www.austinmacauley.com

First Published (2015)
Austin Macauley Publishers Ltd.
25 Canada Square
Canary Wharf
London
E14 5LB

Printed and bound in Great Britain

# Acknowledgments

I wish to thank my wife, Betty, for her encouragement, spell checking and especially for the many hours spent typing my stories.

# 7 DAYS

# ANN'S STORY

My heart is breaking. The man that I love more than life itself has just told me that he does not share my feelings.

He has just walked out the door!

I can feel my heart break.

My name is Ann, I am twenty-two years of age. How can I begin to think of all the empty years to come, without him?

As soon as I saw him I knew he was the ONE.

The differences between us mattered not one jot. He was dancing with Nana at someone's coming home party; six feet tall, lean without being scrawny, with piercing blue eyes and grey hair worn long over his ears in a 1960's style.

I simply could not wait, so I decided that it was an excuse for me to dance – so I did.

His eyes seemed to pour into my soul as I felt weak at the knees.

"My dance, I think," I announced cheekily.

He responded in "olde world" fashion and I was gliding round the floor in his arms.

If I danced a little too closely, he did not seem to notice.

I was carried in a cloud of ecstasy.

He was most polite as he excused himself at the end of the dance, but I was in no doubt that he would not be rushing into another round of the floor.

I cannot begin to describe the feeling of desperation that I experienced as he collected his coat and prepared to leave.

Then exhilaration, Pappy has collected his coat and he and the stranger are leaving. This must be Pappy's old school friend, home from America after forty years.

Then I think that is impossible. Pappy is old, bald, bent and boring: the stranger is straight backed, exuding power and vivacity. He must be twenty years younger than Pappy.

Now I know how to see him again.

# Day 1

I am sitting in Pappy's living room when the front door bell rings.

I almost leap off the chair at its sound and in anticipation of formally meeting the American

Pappy leads the American into the room and announces, "Zack meet my granddaughter, Ann."

I cannot stop the flush spreading up my neck and into my cheeks.

"Pleased to meet you," I manage.

Zack bows slightly takes my hand and says," Pleased to meet you; of course we did meet briefly last night." I am enchanted by his deep baritone voice; slightly Americanised but with a trace of his native country remaining.

I blush again, remembering his body pressed against mine. Or more truthfully, mine pressed against his. I become vaguely aware of Pappy speaking, "Ann would like to accompany us as we relive the old haunts, I hope you don't mind?"

"Charmed I'm sure," responded Zack.

Pappy is speaking again, "Ann is doing some sort of study as part of her degree and wants to record our reactions to our old haunts."

"It's for my Masters," I interject, then realise how childish this makes me seem.

I could have kissed Pappy when he added Nana would be joining us. He asked Zack if he would mind travelling in the back with me as Nana got car sick in the rear.

God bless you Nana, I think.

Zack answers gallantly that he would be honoured to share with me.

Again I blush!

Between old haunts, I quiz him about his life. Following a degree in English he had taken a Masters in American History, then trained as a teacher. At twenty five he had left for America, arriving in New York with only the clothes he stood up in and fifty 'Yankee' dollars.

Two years working on building sites combined with abstemious living enabled him to move south to Maryland and then Virginia.

I listened entranced as he described his work as a tour guide around the battlefields and his feelings about the Civil War. Then he got restless and he moved to North Carolina where he taught English in a College in Hickory.

With obvious embarrassment, Zack described how he met and married the original all singing, all dancing, blue- eyed, blonde all American girl.

Following seven years of 'married bliss' Zack was bored and the all American girl danced off with the Dean of the Faculty.

On his way to College one morning Zack realised that he had nothing to stay for so he kept on walking; all the way to Atlanta, in Georgia. Seven weeks working as a waiter in Atlanta's premier hotel and Zack was ready to move on. Then a guest in the Presidential Suite invited him to come and work for him as his butler, companion and general factotum.

For five years his employer treated him like a son as they travelled the globe. Zack spoke of exciting, scary and amazing places with easy charm.

Then his employer died, leaving Zack a very wealthy man.

It took more than two years to 'sort out' his new estate. The apartment in New York was sold, overseas properties turned into cash and Zack, now a man of leisure moved into his employer's (now his) beach side complex in Miami Beach.

Days running on the beach alongside bronzed beauties all ran into one in an endless round of boredom.

I teased him about all the girls he must have had and I hoped he did not detect the jealousy in my voice.

My heart soared when he emphatically denied my claim. He had been put off marriage for life, now women did not figure in his thinking. "Oh yes," he said, "there had been one or two casual relationships over the years, but never anything serious."

In this sphere alone I was more experienced than Zack. At eighteen I had given my virginity to a school friend so that I could join my girlfriends 'club'. The experience had been fleeting, embarrassing and painful, putting me off sex for several months. Then I met Tom who was a gentle tender lover, always putting my needs first. Always that is, until the next dolly bird came along. Several one night stands finished when I met George. George, one of my lecturers at University. George was everything I had ever wanted and for two years we were gloriously happy. The only down side was that George had to drive home every weekend to see his elderly parents. Despite my every entreaty he refused to bring me home to meet the parents.

Then I discovered WHY! in the shape of a raging demented woman who demanded access to my apartment, claiming George was her husband. He WAS!

I encouraged Zack to tell me what he did next. Two years of boredom upon luxury cruise liners circumnavigating the globe did nothing to alleviate his boredom.

Back home in his beach side mansion Zack tried all sorts of ways to relieve his ennui; shooting in the woods, learning to be a helicopter pilot, then to fly a light plane, but something was always missing.

One night he was flicking through the television channels when he settled on a programme about childhood and adult literacy. The programme claimed that 40-44 million adults were at the lowest level of literacy and a further 50 million at the second lowest level.

Zack had immediately contacted the programme makers, offering a large donation. Though grateful for the money, Zack was informed that it was volunteers and speakers that were required.

For the past twelve years he had travelled the length and breadth of America, speaking at venues to as few as 5 and as many as several thousand people.

I felt so proud of him. Though encased in the back seat of the car I turned round and kissed him on the cheek.

The day had flown by, but I could not bear to be apart from my knight in shining armour. Breathlessly I asked if he would come into 'Uni' to speak to the American Studies and Social Sciences classes.

My delight must have shown as he readily agreed, despite Pappy and Nana's protests, and arrangements were made to meet him at the Faculty entrance at 1pm the day after tomorrow.

I could barely contain my excitement as I drove back to my little apartment. Sleep eluded me as I fantasised about the coming days.

# Day 2

I woke in a cold sweat; I had invited Zack to speak to classes over which I had no control. Nor any meaningful input.

I showered and rushed into work, making sure I was first on the Dean's list of appointees.

Perhaps over excitedly I explained that I had met this famous entrepreneur and philanthropist who was visiting Pappy and who would be willing to speak to the students, free of charge.

The Dean, not unreasonably, asked, "When might this great man be available?"

"Tomorrow," I responded, "he returns to Florida on Sunday."

The Dean played with his computer and seemed pleased by what he read about Zack.

"Alright," he said, "but perhaps more notice in future, young lady."

I had the grace to blush.

The hands of the clock dragged by. I could not wait to see Zack again.

Tomorrow was too far away. I rang Nana to find out if she knew about Zack's whereabouts.

"Of course," she replied, "he and Pappy are fishing and you know they must not be disturbed."

"Nana" I practically begged, "will you ask Zack to ring me when he gets home? I have some stuff I have to discuss with him about tomorrow's classes."

When I switched off the phone I realised that I was shaking. Now I had to think of something to discuss! All evening I sat in nervous anticipation. I knew Pappy and his fishing: it could go on all night. My phone rang nearing 10pm and I practically jumped.

"Hi," the American drawl thrilled in my ear, "I believe you want me."

Oh how I want you, I thought but coolly suggested that I call round to his hotel to discuss the format, attendees and explain about the Dean.

It all sounded so false in my own head. I could quite easily do all this over the phone, but I just had to see him.

Again the drawl, "I'll meet you in the foyer, will I order coffee or something stronger?"

"A gin and tonic always does it for me," I responded. My little Mini never moved as quickly as it did that night.

This time he kissed me on the cheek and we entered a snug. The waiter brought our drinks and some delicate canapés.

"Now let's hear it" Zack drawled, "what is the problem?"

"No problem at all," I answered, "just that you will have more students than I had anticipated."

Zack laughed, "I had anticipated three or four! "No," I replied, "there will be several hundred, I hope you don't mind."

"Of course I don't, I would look forward to it." His look told me my time was up so I blurted out, "I would love to hear more about your philanthropy."

"I would hardly call it philanthropy, but here goes."

A polite cough from the waiter alerted us to the fact that it was 2am and he was going off duty.

Again the music of Zack's laugh stirred me.

"Indeed," he said, looking directly into my eyes "I must have bored you rigid."

"Oh no," I responded too quickly, "I could listen to you all night."

"Then I would be a sorry sight tomorrow" he laughed. I noticed that he laughed a lot.

We stood up to part and impulsively I kissed him on the lips.

Immediately I realised that I had gone too far and apologised for being so 'forward'.

"Not at all," he responded "what is a kiss between friends."

His easy reply had saved the day and definitely saved my face.

Red faced I exited the hotel.

# Day 3

I buzzed about like some demented thing. My colleagues begged me to calm down, Zack was arriving for the 1 o'clock class with open ended time to finish.

Pappy and Nana were taking him to lunch and would drop him off at my office.

How could I be calm?

The large lecture theatre began to fill at 12.30pm and by 12.55pm was packed with students, anxious to hear from this demigod.

Where was Zack? My nerves were on edge. No doubt Pappy was regaling him with one of his stories. At 12.57pm he breezed into my office.

I almost fainted with relief and with something else. There stood my knight in shining armour, dressed in an old denim shirt and tattered Levi jeans, all he lacked were the cowboy boots and the Stetson hat!

"I'm sorry about the attire," he said, "your grandfather was most reluctant to leave the riverside, so I did not have time to change."

Having gulped a couple of times, I rose to the occasion. "You are fine, they are here to listen to what you have to say, not see how you are dressed."

Strangely, he was dressed perfectly. When he entered the lecture theatre with his long hair and faded clothing the student body (to a man and woman) stood and cheered. The Dean seemed to be less impressed. But, in minutes he too was won round.

Zack spoke for 55 minutes, without notes, then invited questions.

At 4.30pm the Dean stood up and interjected, "Sir we must bring this session to a close, otherwise we will be here all night.

Throughout the afternoon I had been filled with pride, love, puppy dog devotion and a host of other emotions. Now I wanted Zack for myself. Alas, it was not to be. Questions, remarks, suggestions continued into the front entrance and out into the quad.

Six pm came and went and by 6.45pm I was becoming quite desperate. Zack was still surrounded by at least 50 students when I brought it all to an end by saying that I had to steal this man away as I had a meal arranged.

Zack seemed reluctant to leave but eventually I got him into the Mini and headed for my favourite restaurant. Before sitting down Zack excused himself saying "I really must have a wash and I'm sure the waiters will not approve of my dress."

I believed he was dressed like a God!

Our meal was divine, served by very discreet waiters. Much to my amazement Zack shared my taste in red wine ordering one and then another of Masi Amarone Classico.

We talked about – I know not what!

The time flew past as I lost myself deeper and deeper in his eyes. I accidently touched his arm, his hand and even brushed against his knee.

Had Zack been worldlier he would have known that I was flirting with him. Throughout the meal he was charming, chatty and paternal.

I did not want paternal, I wanted him! Finally we could remain no longer so I offered to drive him back to his hotel.

My apartment was en-route (nearly) so I invited him up for coffee. It all sounded so contrived. His response startled me as he warmly replied, "I would love to."

I wondered if he realised the significance of my actions. All I knew was that I must have this man. I also realised that flightiness or coquettishness would not lead anywhere.

Zack settled comfortably into 'my chair' as I poured a large brandy for him and got a gin and tonic for myself.

We indulged in small talk. I could wait no longer. I knelt down before him, reached over and kissed him fully on the mouth.

Much to my surprise he responded eagerly, almost desperately.

I do not know how but I found myself in bed with him, experiencing heights that I had never previously known. The world exploded as I experienced my first coital orgasm, followed almost immediately by Zack's climax.

He fell asleep almost immediately. I bathed in the warmth of a 'real man'. His long day perspiration lingered on my body as I lay stroking his iron grey chest hair.

Then I must have slept as I was awakened by the aroma of freshly brewed coffee.

Zack was fully dressed as he approached the bed with two steaming coffee cups. His embarrassment was obvious as he tried to make light of the 'situation'.

"I don't normally do this," he said.

"What"? I asked "make coffee."

"No make love with someone young enough to be my granddaughter."

"I do not normally do this with anyone," I responded.

We both drank our coffees in silence, then he leaned over and kissed me.

I was on fire!

The kiss grew more passionate and soon Zack was undressed and we repeated last night's performance. This time more languorous; the tenderness was palpable.

This was truly 'lovemaking'; deep, meaningful and way beyond lust.

My earlier infatuation blossomed with every movement of our bodies.

Afterwards I told him that I must leave for work but I would like to see him later.

He told me he had a full day's programme with old acquaintances but would return whenever he could.

I showered, gave him a spare key and left for work.

# Day 4

All day I walked around with a smile on my face as my 'insides' tingled with the memory of him. I felt sure that tonight he would tell me that he had fallen in love with me and I would agree to spend the rest of my life with him.

Now, I knew that it was possible to have 'love at first sight'. Wasn't I the living proof of it!

I was certain that my colleagues could tell that we had 'done it', as I hugged myself in secret delight.

I will never know how I got through the day; taking two classes in Social Studies, attending a meeting with my Masters' tutor and writing up student reports.

The day was interminable; just as I was about to leave the Dean sent for me, normally a cause for trepidation. The Dean was effusive about my American friend and seemed in the need for a chat.

Following several skirmishes, beating about the bush and digressions the Dean finally revealed the reason for my visit to his office.

He offered me a Research Fellowship and offered a tiny glass of sherry to mark my elevation.

Now I really had something to celebrate and maybe luck did come in threes: this morning I had Zack, now I had a Fellowship, maybe the third surprise would be an engagement ring?

It wasn't, but the delicate entwined hearts necklace that Zack presented me with went some way towards filling the void. Tonight I did not want to share him with anybody so I ordered a carry out while Zack bought the wine from the off licence.

As we ate (and drank) a furrowed look crossed Zack's brow. "Was last night a one off" he asked, "or is there more?"

"Oh yes there is more; much more" I tell him. I also say that I have never before had this feeling and I had never felt so loved and wanted.

Zack seemed disturbed by practicalities. "But I am much older than you," he said.

"Age means nothing," I retorted.

Zack reminded me that he would be eighty in fifteen years while I would still be in my mid-thirties. I decided to lighten the mood. "But wouldn't it be a wonderful fifteen years!"

"Indeed it would," he responded, wistfully I thought.

Then I just had to say it, "I think I am falling in love with you," I said.

"You must not do that," Zack groaned, "I am going home on Sunday."

"I know," I said "but the world is a small place, there are phones nowadays!"

I wondered why Zack did not laugh. Instead he seemed so sad.

Again I tried to lighten the mood. "Given that the world has not yet ended, do you want to stay or go back to the hotel?"

In that infuriating way with men he answered my question with one of his own. "What do you want?" he asked.

"I want you," I said, which he took to mean that I wanted him to stay.

Which I did. We did not make love that night. He lay with his arms wrapped round me as though he was preventing my escape.

Escape never entered my mind.

His voice grew softer and softer as we drifted off to sleep.

# Day 5

I awake and thank God that this is my last working day, before the weekend. Much as I would have loved to, I could not escape from work as I had pre-arranged student interviews, a tutorial and several records to complete before the weekend.

Zack is sleeping silently beside me. I rise, dress, skip breakfast and leave him a note to have a good day.

Work details escalate and I don't get home until after 7 pm. There is no sign of Zack. I make a light meal, have a bath, and watch some television but still no sign of Zack.

I decide to ring him but realise I do not have the number of his mobile. I cannot ring Nana again, so I try his hotel.

His voice sends a shiver down my spine. "Hi" he says "how are you?"

How am I? I think. I'm mad that he isn't in my flat but I cannot say that.

Instead I say that I thought he might have been here when I got home.

"I did not think you wanted me," he said "you did not invite me round."

I try to control the anger in my voice. "How could I invite you round when you were asleep in my bed when I left?"

"You could have included it in your note."

Normally I would have considered this to be a reasonable response but these were not reasonable times.

I could hear my own voice rise. "Given the fact of how we spent the last two days I do not think an invitation was necessary.

"Indeed," Jack replied "I am most terribly sorry to have offended you. It will not happen again. Goodnight Ann," he concluded.

Oh my God what have I done? Should I pick up the phone and ring back? No, he probably never wants to see me again. What a fool I had been. I picked up the phone, laid it down, threw it in the corner. I paced the room and helped myself to a very large gin and tonic. Finally at 2am I could stand it no longer. I took another bath and retired to my lonely bed. I lay on 'his' side of the bed. I could still smell 'him' on the pillow. I began to cry. I thought that I would cry myself to death.

For the hundredth time I checked the clock; it was after 4am. I checked the phone in case I had put it on silent. I hadn't.

Eventually I fell asleep.

I awake at 9am with a thumping headache, swollen eyes and a deep desire for death.

It is several minutes before I realise that I had been awakened by the sound of the doorbell ringing.

# Day 6

I struggle into my dressing gown, run my fingers through my tousled hair and stumble to the door.

Hesitantly I open up to find the largest bouquet of flowers staring me in the face; the voice from behind the flowers pleads for my forgiveness and adds, "Do you know how hard it is to get a bouquet at this time on a Saturday morning?"

I throw my arms round Zack, spoiling several beautiful flowers in the process.

The flowers are set aside, we are both crying in each other's arms. I catch a glimpse of last night's face and beg to leave to go to the bathroom.

Zack brews coffee as I shower and out on my 'face'. We laugh and cry at our own stupidity as we devour croissants that Zack brought with the flowers.

Breakfast finished, we stood to remove dishes. Zack turned towards me and soon we were engrossed in a passionate kiss.

Whoever said there is no joy like the joy of making up knew what they were talking about. Love making was frantic; hurried, exciting, distraught with fear, anxiety and another unspoken emotion.

Zack begged forgiveness, claiming his lack of experience as a reason for last night's insensitivity.

I remembered and quoted from a line from Love Story; 'love is never having to say you are sorry'.

That strange look reappeared in Zack's eyes but I put it down to anxiety.

We lay holding each other tightly and then I felt Zack becoming aroused again. I marvelled that a man of sixty five had such sexual stamina; more than enough for me.

We made love with great gentility, treasuring every moment as if it were the last. Afterwards Zack reminded me of the party at Pappy's house planned for tonight. If there was anything I wished to do we had only four or five hours left in which to do it.

I did not want to do anything other than hold him as if my life depended on it; and I truly believed that it did.

We closed the curtains, sitting in semi-darkness, occasionally having coffee but mainly just holding each other.

Then it was 7 o'clock and time for Zack to go. We cried some more, knowing that we could not spend this last night alone together. Zack suggested that we might try to be alone in a crowd at tonight's party.

I cried anyway.

By 9 o'clock I had recovered sufficiently enough to drive to Pappy's house.

I find Zack just as I found him one week ago dancing with Nana. "Excuse me," I say "my dance I believe," and I am in his arms. I can hear Nana's less than subtle comment to Pappy, "We will have to watch that one. She is out to get Zack." We pretend not to hear her.

The night is centred on Zack, so I have little time with him, yet he returns to me at every opportunity for yet another 'last dance'.

At midnight the party begins to break up and I must leave. Zack is spending his last night with his old friend Pappy, and I must go home.

Zack escorts me to the door and kisses me goodbye. He whispers, urgently "I think I will get away early from here and call with you in the morning before I get my flight."

I can barely see through my tears and his voice feels that it is coming from a long way away.

And tomorrow, that is exactly how it will be, Zack will be a long way away.

The Mini drives itself home.

On automatic pilot I undress, shower and prepare for bed.

# Day 7

The doorbell rings at 8 o'clock and I have been awake for hours.

The Zack that stands before me is not my 'cowboy' nor my 'knight in shining armour'. This Zack is expensively dressed in a Savile Row suit, shirt and shoes from Jermyn Street and old school tie: his hair is combed back and he oozes wealth. Yet beneath it all he is still my Zack.

This Zack is the successful philanthropist, sure of his every move. He sits down in my (his) chair.

Without preamble he begins, "Ann, whatever is between us cannot go on. We can have no future together, I cannot give you what you want, I cannot love you the same way you love me. Whatever we had is over. If I hurt you I am sorry."

He rose and walked out the door without looking back.

My heart is breaking: the man that I love more than life itself has just told me that he does not share my feelings.

My heart is breaking: without him there is no life, no existence.

My steps are purposeful: first the medicine cupboard then the drinks cabinet.

I carefully count out the tablets, pour my drink, backed up by a pint glass of water.

Nothing must prevent what must happen.

# Zack's Story

## Day 1

I was quite surprised to find my 'dancing partner' from last night sitting in David's kitchen.

The surprises continued when David introduced Ann, as his granddaughter and announced that she would be accompanying us today.

Good manners prevented me from saying that I would have liked to visit our old haunts with just David. After all, those childhood memories belonged to him and me and not to his granddaughter. Then Jean announced her intentions to join us and I am relegated to the back seat with Ann.

I struggle to contain my resentment as I can see little of the scenery from the rear of the car. Not only can I not see the scenery, I am bombarded with personal questions from the seemingly endless optimistic and outgoing Ann. As she seeks to discover my soul her left leg is pressed firmly against my right one. I am engulfed by mixed emotions, could a 22 year old be attracted to an elderly man. I question myself as to whether her leg is caressing mine or if I am imagining things.

I chastise myself not to be so ridiculous, what would this flame haired beauty see in me, yet the pressure persists. As the day went on the questions became increasingly more personal.

Was she so insensitive that she could not see that her questions were causing great embarrassment? I was aware of David and Jean's listening ears in the front seats and resolved to say as little as possible about my 'love life' in which their granddaughter was so interested.

White lie followed white lie followed whopper. Surely she could not believe that a sixty five year old, foot loose, wealthy man would not have his fair share of women.

Silently I begged forgiveness from my ex-wife for accusing her of running off with the Dean. She had abandoned the marital bed but only after finding me in it with someone else. I condoned this lie by telling myself that I did not want David or Jean to think ill of me. At some level I must have been aware that I wanted Ann to think well of me too. And where was the harm in making my life seem more interesting that it really had been.

Anyway it was true that I ended up as the confidant and adopted son of a very rich man. It was also true that my inheritance was in the hundreds of millions of dollars. And I really did contribute millions to try and improve literacy in the States; where my ideas took flight of fancy was in my twelve year commitment to the cause. In truth I attended half a dozen black tie dinners each year and spoke at Universities and Colleges four or five times a year.

The way I told it, I was a cross between Mother Theresa and Archbishop Desmond Tutu and the granddaughter seemed mighty impressed.

For that matter so did David and Jean. I was secretly pleased with myself knowing the story would be extended in the retelling.

Ann hinted to me that she had a colourful life but I put my hand to her mouth exhorting her to hold her counsel. I was beginning to think that things had changed since I left the 'old country' where a young girl could talk about her sex life in front of others; especially her grandparents.

I think I hid my annoyance at being denied my old memories very well as Ann asked if I would speak to members of her faculty in a couple of days.

I have always found it hard to say no to requests and impossible to refuse a beautiful woman, so I acquiesced.

I must confess to a feeling of relief from the interrogation when Ann left. David and I then did what we should have done all day; we reminisced over several large brandies and planned for the day's fishing next day.

# Day 2

The ideal day for fishermen; not too bright, clouds overhead with plenty of shade. Jean had prepared a hamper to sustain David and me throughout the day. David very kindly insisted that I should have his best rod and reel as we sought out the river for a day of fly fishing.

To the casual observer fishing is a leisure activity conducted by fat men sitting by a riverbank quaffing cans of beer.

For serious fishermen, such as David and myself, it is a war fought between man and fish. We take our fishing seriously, approaching it as a science that requires attention, a positive attitude, accuracy in casting, acceptance of all aspects of the battle, coupled with endless patience.

The day started well enough, with a few trial casts to find where the fish were biting; we selected our spots and the serious business began. Or at least it did for David. I found my attention being drawn from the task at hand to images of red gold hair, emerald green eyes and habitual flicking of her fringe.

I shake myself back to the present, chiding myself for being a silly old fool. After all she is only twenty two! My positive attitude is undermined by my fevered imagination as I metaphorically run my hand through her long, lovely hair. I ask myself why I am so obsessed when yesterday, I was irritated by her endless questions? I have no answer.

I shake myself back to the present as David proudly displays his first catch of the day; a fine trout that is nearly one pound in weight. I smile congratulations and return to the task in hand. Once more I find my arm is way off as I cast towards my target. So much for accuracy, I think, as my mind returns to the beautiful Ann.

Suddenly she has become a water nymph, dancing on the limpid stream. She turns, shakes her golden hair and smiles towards me.

I find myself accepting that my fishing is spoiled by my obsession. I suggest lunch and David unpacks Jean's spread.

We sit, reliving old memories, mainly those that never really happened. The sun is high in the sky, not a shadow on the water and the flies in abundance.

The fish are not biting so we relax, eat, talk and drift into sleep.

Soon David is snoring peacefully, as I drift off into her world. We are walking hand in hand along Miami Beach, throwing stones for the dog to fetch. She looks into my eyes and I move forward to kiss her.

Just then I am dragged back to the riverside as David announces that it is time restart. The sun has moved across the sky and the fish are biting.

David manages to catch three more fine trout while I snag trees, allow my fly to sink and generally fish like a beginner.

Unsurprisingly, my bag is empty at the end of the day and David suggests a pub visit to console me. A couple of scotches later and appetite stimulated, we stay for dinner, not getting back to the hotel until nearly 10 o'clock.

David drops me off, having arranged some coarse fishing for the following morning.

I have just stripped off my old clothes in preparation for a shower when the phone rings. Jean tells me that I should phone Ann about some details regarding tomorrow's talk.

She must have had the phone right beside her as she answered at the first ring. We exchanged pleasantries, then she suggested coming to the hotel to discuss some issues.

Despite prompting from me, Ann seemed reluctant to discuss her issues over the phone, so I arranged to meet her in the foyer.

She arrived in a great bustle, bouncing through the foyer, wild hair flowing behind her.

I kiss her on the cheek and organise drinks and canapés.

We move to a snug and the waiter brings our drinks. Ann outlines her issues; all of which could have been dealt with over the phone. Then she recommences her questioning. Again I supress my irritation about discussing areas of my private life that have long been locked away.

At 2am the waiter indicated the need for us to leave so that he could go home.

I stand, escort Ann to the front door and prepare to say goodbye.

My surprise is obvious when Ann stands on her tiptoes and kisses my lips.

My lips are on fire, my heart thuds in my chest but Ann apologises.

I laugh it off and we arrange to meet before 1pm tomorrow.

# Day 3

Room service rings at 7.30am to inform me that I have a visitor in the foyer.

I leap out of bed, in alarm, pull on a pair of jeans and a denim shirt. I search desperately for my shoes and settle for my ancient moccasins.

I stumble into the lift and on exit in the foyer apologise profusely to David who is suitably kitted out for the morning 'fish'.

David laughs at my discomfort, assuring me that he has an old jacket and wellington boots in the car. We have hasty coffees, then we are off to the riverbank.

Again I apologise to David, laying the blame squarely on the shoulders of his granddaughter. I complain she kept me talking until 2am and I was no longer fit for late nights.

David laughed, and together we cursed advancing age. In truth I was glad to say her name as the memory of her kiss lingered on my lips.

The chosen venue was some distance away and David was keen to get started before the sun got too high. We fished solidly for two hours. This was truly the layperson's image of fishing; two old blokes sitting by the river with fishing rods clamped to the ground. With great skill and dexterity we managed to catch – Nothing!

David opened Jean's freshly made brunch which we enjoyed immensely along with a couple of warm beers. The sun took its toll and again we dozed off. For the second time today I woke with a great start, checked the time and jumped to my feet. "David" I yelled "it is ten past twelve and I am due at the University at 1pm!

David was infuriating in his lack of haste. Slowly, oh so slowly, he gathered the fishing tackle and threw it in the boot.

I removed my jacket and wellies, which joined the tackle in the boot. David began to drive back.

"We do not have time to go to the hotel, you will have to meet Ann in the clothes you have on." I groan inwardly. What will the students think? I am the archetypical middle (old) aged hippy in denims, moccasins and no socks!

Panic sets in, what will Ann think?

Ann disguises her shock very well, as I arrive with two or three minutes to spare.

I have no idea what Ann had told the students about me; perhaps an ageing hobo, a Box Car Willie? Whatever she had said I was greeted like a returning hero. I turned round to see if Willie Nelson had arrived behind me.

An elderly chap (about my age) sat in the front row. His response did nothing to encourage me. I assumed this was the Dean who looked on in disgust.

I begin my talk and soon I am on automatic pilot. I notice the Dean is smiling and clapping as loudly as everyone else.

I catch a glimpse of Ann, smiling at the side of the stage. The question and answer session is even better than the talk and continues out into the quad. It is with mixed feelings that I allow Ann to 'drag' me away for dinner.

I am on such a fantastic high that I have no idea what we ate or drank and I am only vaguely aware of Ann's topics of conversation.

I am acutely aware of the subtle perfume that drifts across and I am tempted to reach out and take her hand as she flicks back a non-existent stray hair.

Throughout the meal and over brandies she reaches out often and touches my hand, my wrists and my arms. Occasionally her knee touches mine, sending electric shocks throughout my body.

The atmosphere is electric, or is it simply the imaginings of a silly old man. I determine to be reserved.

The evening comes to an end and Ann offers to drive me to my hotel. God knows I need to be there; a morning by the river, an afternoon in a lecture theatre and an evening in an overheated restaurant has done little to improve my 'man smells'.

On our way home Ann invites me up to her place for coffee. I wonder vacantly if such an invite has the same inference here as it does in the States!

I make myself comfortable as Ann gets the drinks. I sip my brandy and set the glass on the table beside me.

In a dream or fugue, I see Ann kneel before me and her lips are on mine.

This time I respond desperately as our needs carry us into the bedroom. Ann throws of her clothes as I, gingerly, remove my sweat stained shirt and pants praying that she won't be put off by my body odour.

She isn't, and I bring a lifetime of practiced seduction to bear, fondling, kissing, licking, squeezing and entering with great thrusts.

Mentally I follow Ann's every move 'playing her like a great conductor'. Ann explodes in ecstasy and for the first time in my entire life I lose control and explode almost immediately.

My last thoughts as I drift off to sleep are the hopes that she had not detected my lies about lack of sexual experience. She begins to caress my now saturated chest hairs.

As is normal for me I awake early, slip out of bed as quietly as possible. I put the dirty clothes back on my now clean body and move to the kitchen where I manage to make two cups of coffee.

With a degree of embarrassment that I have not experienced for forty years I approach the bed and offer Ann a cup.

She obviously detects my embarrassment and indulges in some light banter.

We finish our coffees and I lean across the bed to kiss Ann goodbye. Her tongue is in my mouth and I am on fire, I feel the old familiar feeling in my groin and stumble into bed. This time the lovemaking is tender, passionate and honest, I am not leading, not guiding nor controlling. I am lost in the moment: well in many moments as we carry our lovemaking to fruition. Reluctantly we leave the bed, Ann showers and gets ready to go to work.

I make more coffee and we agree to meet later.

# Day 4

My day is taken up with pre-arranged meetings. First a visit to my old school: having gone back to the hotel to change into more appropriate clothing. I recount to the children my memories of my time in the school, but all they wanted to hear is 'all about America'. One freckled face lad puts his hand up and demands, "Is it true that all Americans are millionaires?" I assure him it is not and I describe the poverty in which many exist.

A pretty little blue eyed blonde pipes up," But you are rich, aren't you?"

"I suppose I am," I responded and the little coquette adds, "Then I can marry you when I grow up!"

This elicits much laughter and all too soon it is time to go.

I trade one educational establishment for another as I taxi across to my old University. Some of my old classmates now lecture there, so we have a nostalgic lunch prior to meeting more students.

One enterprising undergraduate had looked me up on the Internet. "Is it true," he asked "that you are a worth a billion dollars?"

"Not quite," I answer "but I am comfortably off."

Like universities and colleges the world over, there is always at least one belligerent student, and this place was no different.

"What do you do with your money?" he demanded aggressively.

So I give an exaggerated version of my good works with America's underclasses, particularly regarding literacy.

The class erupted in a massive round of applause but our belligerent one was not finished.

"So you give your time, but how much money do you give to the cause?"

I could feel my colour heighten as I responded, "To date about $100million and they will benefit massively when I die." These figures silenced my critic and energised the remainder. The cheers and hand clapping lasted for a full five minutes.

Then it was time for tea with cousins, aunties, uncles, neighbours and friends. As I sipped the weak tea I wondered what Ann was doing.

There is no way to contact her. I must just soldier on until it is time to return to her apartment. Two hours is more than enough with my kinfolk, so I call in with David and Jean.

As I sip much better tea I realise that I have an errand to do before meeting Ann. Besides I do feel guilty sitting here with the grandparents, having recently made love to their granddaughter.

At the jewellers I search in vain for an appropriate present. I explained to the jeweller that I wanted something unique and he, laughing, suggests an engagement ring. Too early or too late for that I think and continue my search.

Having exhausted myself and the jeweller I turned to leave the shop. I am stopped by "ah ha!" from the jeweller. "I may have the very thing, if it is unique that you want." "I do indeed" I replied and the jeweller goes into the back room, returning with a blue satin box embossed with gold filigree.

The jeweller opens the box with an exaggerated flair, to reveal a necklace with entwined hearts, each strand of the necklace is also entwined with hearts and the hearts consist of flashing emeralds.

"I like it," I say, "but I would prefer gold to silver."

"My dear Sir," the jeweller exclaimed, "the silver is platinum and your young lady will love it."

"Ok "I say, "I'll take it."

The jeweller wraps his sale without ever mentioning the price. I proffer my American Express card which informs him there is no limit. He is suitably impressed as he hands me my purchase and a receipt for £10,000.

I seek reassurance and he tells me my friend will love it.

And she does!

Back at Ann's apartment, she is stunned by her present but declines my offer to eat out.

As Ann rings for a carry out I go to the off licence buying six of their best bottles of wine. On my return Ann laughs and opines that she hoped that we were not going to drink it all at once.

Over dinner and the fine wine Ann is strangely quiet and I worry that she is regretting our love making. Her reply was more than I could cope with. This beautiful young woman is telling me that I am the love of her life!

I remind her that I am old enough to be her father /grandfather. Ann laughs, "But age has no bearing on our feelings."

Quite reasonably I tell her that I am nearer to eighty than she is to forty. But nothing would deter her. She would have her way; 'she loved me'. Several times I came close to telling her that I felt exactly the same way, but good sense prevailed and I held my counsel.

When she asked me if I wanted to stay the night I felt compelled to ask her if she wanted me to stay. I was all too aware that I had failed to utter those magic three words 'I love you'. Despite my omission she still wanted my company. We did not make love, but in many ways the night was best of all. I lay holding her near, hyper aware of her breathing, of the rise and fall of her breasts. Words were unnecessary as our souls fused together.

# Day 5

When I awake she is gone. A brief note tells me to have a good day. There is no invitation for this evening and no mention of last night.

A deep loneliness returns as I reason that she has had enough of me.

I rise, shower and leave, returning to my hotel about 9am.

I shower again in my room and change into fresh clothing. The phone rings but it is not her. It is an old friend inviting me for lunch. I check my diary, which is free but tell him, "Sorry I am tied up maybe next time."

"Of course," he responds and wishes me a safe journey home. I ring David and cancel our planned outing on his boat. I plead a headache. David is most concerned, inviting me round to stay with him and Jean. He assures me Jean is an excellent nurse but I refuse his kind offer. I have lunch delivered to my room and decide to have an afternoon nap. I cannot sleep, I resolve to ring Ann to find out what is the problem.

Then I realise that I do not know her number and I certainly cannot ring David.

At 4 o'clock I venture out and walk for miles. I gaze blindly into shop windows. I speak to no one and avoid eye contact with all other pedestrians. I return to have dinner in my room.

I ask if I have had any calls and am surprised when she says, "No!"

I am sitting contemplating going to bed when the phone rings.

"Hi," I say and wait for the caller to speak.

"Hello," she says very quietly.

"Oh hi," I say "how are you?"

Her voice sounds offended. "I thought you would be here when I got home."

I am gobsmacked and remind her that she did not invite me. The anger in her voice is patent as she reminds me of our interactions over the previous two days. "I would have thought an invitation was unnecessary."

I waited for more but nothing was forthcoming.

It is much too late to go round to her apartment so I apologise profusely. I tell her that I am most terribly sorry for having offended her and assure her that it won't happen again.

With as loving a voice as I could muster I say, "Goodnight Ann" and put down the phone.

# Day 6

I awaken early, dress in my best smart casuals, hurry breakfast and rush out to find a florist. There are no twenty four hour florists here so I walk aimlessly until the shop opens at 9am.

I buy the largest bouquet that I can manage to carry and take a taxi round to her apartment.

When she opens the door it is obvious that she has been crying but she has never looked lovelier. I take her in my arms; it might have been better to have set down the flowers!

There we are, crying like children in each other's arms. Both of us make an earth shattering discovery that we are starving. Coffee and croissants take care of the hunger, only to be replaced by another one. I must have her, somehow I know that our lovemaking will undo all the hurt. I beg forgiveness and she quotes from one of her favourite films.

I amaze myself with the strength of my longing. Twice in two hours we make love. First with anxiety, excitement and some level of fear; then secondly very gently and with deep love and compassion. We spend all day in Ann's apartment, then I remind her of the party that her Pappy has laid on for me.

At 7pm I kiss her tenderly and tell her that I will see her in a couple of hours. I must rush round to my hotel, shower and change for the party.

I am dancing with Jean when history repeats itself. Ann steps forward and announces that this is an 'excuse me' dance and soon she is gliding round in my arms.

All evening others made demands on my time but I returned to dance with Ann at every opportunity. I was aware of all the eyes upon us as we took to the floor but I was past caring what people thought.

At midnight I escort Ann to the door and whisper that I will come round and see her in the morning before my flight.

I have every intention of asking her to marry me! David keeps me awake all night reminiscing about the old days and it is almost 2am by the time I get to bed.

I start to plan my proposal, then reality kicks in. It is impossible. I cannot give her a future that she deserves. I am too old, too set in my ways, too many ghosts reaching out from the past.

No, I must follow a different path.

It is still dark when I slip out of David's house. I leave a note for David and Jean, expressing my gratitude for all that they had done for me.

I walk to my hotel, pack, get dressed and prepare for my final meeting with Ann.

# Day 7

My heart is breaking. I have just lied to the only woman that I have truly loved. I told her that I did not love her in the way she loves me.

I feel my heart break as I walk out the door. My name is Zack and I am sixty five years old. The cancer that I have been fighting for five years has won.

I number my life in days; six or seven weeks at most.

I am home for one last visit, much against the Consultant's advice.

She crashed into my life in a flurry of flaming red hair, dirndl dress and flashing green eyes.

My home coming party was incredibly boring; I knew no one but my old school friend and his wife. As I was dancing with her I was suddenly accosted by a demand to dance.

I continued to waltz with my new partner dancing much too intimately for my liking.

At the end of the dance I thanked her politely and escaped back to my friend and his wife.

Without being aware of 'why', I felt somewhat uneasy as the old familiar empty feeling crept into my soul.

My friend suggested an early escape to his house where we could have a nightcap before I returned to my hotel. We made our escape, but the strangest seven days of my life were just beginning. Seven days in the last seven weeks!

I have just left her having told her that I do not share her feelings. In truth I am enchanted but how can I speak of that when I have so little time.

In a day or two she will receive my letter explaining everything. By then I will have revised my will and she shall be a very rich woman. I hope my riches compensate her, in some way, for the hurt I have caused.

As my flight circles above her I recall every moment, these will be my last memories.

# A Forbidden Love

Sandra and Peter had been married for fifteen years when they finally accepted that there would be no children by 'natural means'. Private consultants and IVF with all its embarrassments proved unproductive. Sandra and Peter agreed surrogacy was out of the question. Well informed relatives were certain that the pair were too old to adopt babies; perhaps older children might be available to them.

In her own pragmatic way, Sandra was adamant that there were babies somewhere for them. It was just a matter of finding them.

Fate intervened through a personal column in a Turkish paper while the pair were on holiday in that country. Sandra wanted a boy and Peter wanted a girl!

After much discussion the would-be parents agreed they could have both. Following endless bureaucratic bungles, hiccups and sheer bloody mindedness by officials Peter and Sandra had their babies.

Back home, the babies were shown off to all and sundry who 'billed and cooed' over them. Twins they were not: She was small, petite, and blonde to almost albino, with the palest of blue eyes. He was black as night, with expressive chocolate eyes and a sturdy body. As the neighbours cooed they privately muttered that there would be trouble ahead. The little ones were just too different in every way, there could be no happy ending.

Sandra detected their reservations but was determined to pour all her love into them; then everything would be just fine. The babies' beds were placed alongside each other; each with their own hot water bottle and blanket and a soft light overhead in case they feared the dark.

Peter and Sandra took one last look at Sam and Grace (for that was their new names). Softly Sandra whispered, "Look how they are lying." Sam lay on his left side as if he were gazing at Grace, while she lay on her right side gazing back.

That was how they slept every night until they were more active.

Again it was Sandra who detected a change in sleeping arrangements. One night, as she looked in, she noticed that Grace had sneaked into Sam's bed and they were now fast asleep in a warm embrace.

Thinking it would do no harm she left them together.

As Sam and Grace grew they were inseparable. They appeared to be fulfilled by their own company, never seeking others as playmates.

The togetherness continued all through their schooling. Others in their class may have considered them to be aloof and stand offish. Neither Sam nor Grace cared. They had each other.

On days when Peter took Sam to help him on the farm, Grace mooched around, like a lost sheep, until their return. Then she would run and meet Sam at the doorway, looking lovingly up into his eyes.

As the years passed and larger beds were required Sam and Grace moved into their separate rooms but their closeness continued. Sam was the epitome of good manners, stepping back to allow Grace to be first for breakfast. She, in turn, would gaze into those deep brown eyes and silently offer Sam her leftovers.

While Sandra and Peter were pleased with the almost psychic powers that Sam and Grace possessed, neighbours expressed concern at their closeness. One neighbour went so far as to say that the relationship was unnatural but he knew a therapist who could help.

Neither Peter nor Sandra believed that there was a problem but agreed that seeing a behavioural therapist could do no harm.

When the therapist arrived he found Sam on the settee watching television with Grace lying with her head on his shoulder.

The therapist took one long look and muttered, "There is nothing I can do. Obviously 'imprinting' has been deep and protracted." He added, "I am attending a convention next week and I will ask my colleagues if they have ever experienced such rapport between a collie and a cat!"

# A Hard World

Vicky's mother died five minutes after she was born. It had always been the plan that Vicky would be the last but it was not meant to work out like this.

All named after the Queens of England, Mary, Elizabeth, and Anne were all under five years old. They had laughed that Victoria would complete the set.

Granda Ted and Granny Rose had been in attendance when Katherine breathed her last. Words had been unnecessary as a look of sorrow passed between son and mother. Granny Rose gently took the new born infant.

Granda Ted rummaged in the loft extracting Jim's old cot which he placed beside the bed in their room. Jim had more than enough on his hands; they would provide all the love and care the infant needed.

Feeding bottles were sterilized, teats purchased and professional advice sought regarding feeding regimes.

In the beginning Ted and Rose took it in turns to do the bottle feeding during the night. Rose was chief carer during the day while Ted busied himself at work. Jim called daily to see the waif who thrived under the loving attention.

In due course Vicky moved into her own room but there was never any doubt as to who 'ruled the roost'.

Ted and Rose had adopted the role of Da and Ma and while she loved Da it was Ma that she always called for when there was worry or things to frighten her.

Seasons came and went and Vicky's beauty was soon commented upon by all who met her. Some said she was the image of her mother while others remarked that she reminded them of her grandmother when she was young. Ted and Rose loved all the attention given to their little darling. For years now Rose referred to her as her 'darling princess' while to Ted she was his 'little lamb'.

Full grown now, Ted and Rose knew that the time would soon come to part with their darling Vicky. How they longed to hold on to her for as long as possible but the suitors' came calling.

Jim was first to discover that Vicky was pregnant and ultrasound confirmed that she was expecting twins.

The father disappeared from the scene shortly before the twins were born, leaving Vicky all alone and bereft.

Ted sought Rose's advice regarding providing a home for Vicky and the twins and was delighted when she agreed.

Night and day he toiled in the building that abutted their house, making it into a comfortable home for the little family. At last he expressed himself satisfied and sought Rose's approval. As with all women, Rose felt the need to add a woman's touch, making the new abode warm and comfortable. In time the twins were born and in accordance with family tradition they were named after the Queens of England. The first born was named Charlotte, wife of George the third and the second Jane after Jane Seymour, third wife of Henry the eighth.

As Ted, Rose and Jim gazed at the newborns they had but a single thought; what a grand family of Royals. In due course they would get to see Mary, Elizabeth and Anne and what a Royal gathering that would be.

In no time at all the twins were spending more time in Ma and Pa's house than their own. Ted blamed Rose for encouraging them into the house and Vicky did nothing to keep them at home. As Ted was fond of remarking, 'it was hardly worth his time and expense making a home for them next door!' Apart from sleeping in their own home, the girls spent all their time with Rose and Ted.

The twins were about five months old when the local butcher called to see Ted and Rose. He cast an appreciative eye over mother and daughters as they played in the orchard. Turning to Ted he said, "I can give you top dollar for Charlotte and Jane but Vicky won't fetch much." He went on to say that the price of mutton had fallen dramatically. He offered a price. Ted looked at Rose; Rose nodded!

# Amazing Grace

Let me tell you, my friend, having a much younger partner isn't all it is 'cracked up' to be. Yes, yes, I hear you laugh but it does have its down sides.

Granted all my middle aged friends cackle at my good luck. There is much 'nudge, nudge and wink, winking,' and my best friend claims that she and I have nothing to talk about! No doubt he is right as her interests are so different to mine. I am serious, settled into middle age and mainly interested in reading and intellectual pursuits. She is young, vivacious, and flirtatious and very definitely has a mind of her own. I suppose it has worked, so far, as she does her thing and I do mine.

Grace has been with me for more than four years. When we met I had not long been divorced and she was on her own. Friends pointed out that the relationship couldn't possibly work; I was forty, too set in my ways, grumpy and, according to my ex-wife, incapable of loving anyone but myself. I could find no argument with my 'ex's' reasoning.

When I tell my friends that it was Grace who 'hit on me' they laugh raucously and who can blame them. Grace is aptly named, exuding grace, elegance and beauty; if others say she is haughty and stand-offish I can only pity their lack of perception.

As I have already said, it was Grace who 'hit on me'. I was returning home, quite intoxicated, from yet another drunken spree when I spotted her standing just outside my driveway.

Perhaps standing is not the best description, lounging or loitering insolently in that horrible adolescent way would be a more accurate description.

Fearing that I was going to be attacked I did what all alpha males do when they are scared, I yelled at her to clear off. She looked at me with distain before hopping on to the garden wall.

"Clear off," I repeated but made the mistake of looking into her eyes. It was thunderbolt time and she knew it.

I knew it was wrong from the start but when she walked with me to the front door I made no objections. Even as I turned the key in the lock, I was telling myself I did not want any of the responsibilities that accompanied a new relationship. Not a word was spoken as I opened the door and let her enter the house.

That was four years ago and nothing has been the same since. Eating habits have changed, meals being dictated by her wishes. We retire when she wants, go out when she demands it and play when she is in the mood.

Obviously there are compensations. As I look at her now, lying with her head on my lap, watching television I am overwhelmed with love.

But, dear friend, it is not always like this. Grace has very definite ideas about how life should be lived. When she wants to go out at night, without me, she simply ignores my pleas to stay with me. At times like this she is inscrutable and I believe she is daring me to end our relationship.

I rage about her behaviour; I would never have accepted it from my ex-wife or previous girlfriends. But Grace is oblivious to my jealousy, she simply takes leave of me as and when she wishes. I usually stay up until midnight, hoping she will return and wondering who she is with.

My best mate laughs at my discomfiture, claiming 'young ones' need their nights on the tiles. His mocking laughter does nothing to make me feel any better. With advancing middle age I need my sleep, so I slip off to bed with the intention of reading until she returns. I am resolute that I will tell her that I can no longer put up with her thoughtless behaviour. I will finish it tonight.

Then I awaken to find her lying in bed beside me, huge eyes staring into mine and I am lost all over again. I don't even ask what time she got home, restricting myself to inanities. I offer to make breakfast. Not only does she eat her own, soon she is helping me eat my bacon and eggs. I wonder how she stays so slim with that voracious appetite. She just looks at me in her mysterious way and I fall in love once more. Falling in love with Grace happens a dozen times a day, usually when she performs some small act of kindness.

My friend, even though I fall in love with her every day, there are also times when I could cheerfully throttle her; none more so than when she reminds me of her youth and my advancing years.

Let me tell you of one example, my friend; on our way into town there are a series of steps and handrails leading down into the town centre. As I start my descent, holding on to the hand rail, she stands at the top step grinning fiendishly. There she stands until I am half way down the first flight of steps, then she bounds past me, waiting for me at the bottom. She repeats this process down all three sets of steps and I swear she laughs at my discomfort. To add insult to injury she skips off on her own as I make my way gingerly around the shops.

That, my friend, is but one example of the difficulties of my situation. But what can I do, I am hopelessly, helplessly in love with her?

Yes, yes I know it is quite likely that she does not love me as I love her, but she really is the most beautiful cat in the world and my life would be empty without her.

# Darkness Falls 1

Darkness falls. As the last vestige of light fades from the autumn sky, he silently rises from his resting place. His first movements are tentative, emerging slowly from the partially open grave.

The cemetery is several hundred years old, overgrown with ferns; shrubs and bushes run wild. One hundred years have passed since the last internment in this place which suits him perfectly.

He has lain here daily for several months, hidden from the light of day. As night falls he emerges, ghost like from the long abandoned grave. Whoever resided here before him is long gone and he has 'homefied' the space to his own liking. Over the months he has spent every night in fruitful preparation. He knows every trail, every hidden nook and more importantly every hidden danger.

He shivers involuntarily every time he passes the disused church with its crumbling crucifix. On moonlit nights the shadow from the crucifix falls across his pathway to the entrance way, forcing him to find a longer, more dangerous path into the houses that surround the cemetery.

But tonight there is no moonlight, his world is as dark as sin; yet there are dangers.

Though there are no relatives left alive to visit their deceased families, others come to the haunted place. He has witnessed young lovers, occasionally thinking of making their acquaintance.

More annoyingly hordes of teenage thugs have frequently turned his home into a drinking den. Their behaviour lacks grace and refinement as they desecrate this so called 'sacred place'.

From his shelter he has watched these hoodlums smash beer bottles, drink to excess and be sick amongst the graves as they bellow in their coarse and crude language.

Worst of all, he has seen them go on rampages smashing grave stones, breaking windows and exposing long dead remains to the elements.

Not that he cares about religious practices or their icons. He does worry though that they might stumble upon his resting place at the most secluded part of the cemetery. But he has chosen well; his home is immediately beneath an ancient Yew tree whose branches shelter and hide his presence. Dense shrubbery and brambles serve to further protect his sanctuary.

He watches furtively from the undergrowth as the teenagers come to the end of their revels. He has chosen his target.

Most scruffy and most careless among the group are the Thompson twins. They live just across the road from the cemetery and he has seen the state of their bedroom. Despite their mother's desperate pleas there are clothes scattered everywhere; crumbs, potato crisps and half eaten biscuits are strewn around the room.

He has watched from the shadows as the twins carried midnight feasts to their room. Doubtless tonight would be no different from all the others; soon wrappers, more crumbs and half-finished glasses of milk would turn the bedroom into a shambles.

He watches as they climb the stairs.

He waits for ten or fifteen minutes, following the switch off of the lights then makes his entrance.

It takes but a moment to access the bedroom. He waits, listening for the heavy breathing of sleep.

His heart beat increases, this is his moment as he prepares for his feast. Then horror of horrors someone flicks on the bedside light.

"Mum, Mum," they yell, "come quickly, there is a mouse in the room!"

He scurries beneath the floorboards.

# Darkness Falls 2

Darkness falls. The night air crackles with tension.

The moment they had waited for, for so long, was almost upon them. Silently the Sergeant ghost walked from man to man, checking that all was in order; properly blacked up, boots buffed to remove the shine and luminous watches covered with tape. It was imperative that the troop remained invisible to the very last second.

Using hand signals the Sergeant ascertained that all men were sure of their impending roles. Working on the premise that there is always one more thing to do, he retraced his footsteps, checking and rechecking.

Twenty years in the army does that to a man. Service at home and in many of the world's trouble spots had taught him that 'one cannot be too careful'. He could feel the men grow impatient for the coming action. It was ever so; nervous men becoming edgy in anticipation of an uncertain future.

Still he held off, as the moon threw her light over the open ground before them. This was where most danger lay, this was the place where they were most likely to be spotted.

The Corporal whispered, "Can we move Sarge, the men are getting restless?"

The Sergeant shook his head, pointing upwards, "That cloud will cover the moon in five minutes. Tell the men to be ready to move. Move out singly, keeping ten yards apart. We will regroup at the other side."

The Corporal relayed the message and each man made his preparation in his own way.

"Go," the Sergeant tapped the first man on the shoulder, "follow the hedge line, keeping out of the light."

Ten times he issued this command, then spoke to the Corporal, "Time for you Corporal and good luck. With any luck I will be with you in a few minutes."

"Thank you Sir," whispered the Corporal as he began his journey.

The Sergeant sought out some brushwood and swept their hiding place. As far as he could see he had left no evidence of their presence.

Time to go, then the moon came out. Cursing his luck, the Sergeant dropped to the ground and monkey crawled all the way to his men.

Rising exhausted, he gasped, "We'll wait here for two minutes until I recover, then we will be on our way."

Not only does fortune favour the brave, it also favours the lucky. And this night they are lucky, a bank of cloud almost totally obliterates the moon. They proceed in almost total darkness until the Sergeant gives the universal signal to stop.

Silently he points straight ahead, "There is our target but first we have to cross the road."

He sends a senior Private forward to recce.

The Private reports back that all is clear, there is cover almost opposite the target and a large hiding place on the far side of the road. Cautiously they make their move. Soon the Sergeant, Corporal and ten Other Ranks are hidden directly across the road from the target.

The Sergeant points to an outbuilding just south of the target. "One by one," he whispers. "If any traffic appears make a run for it. In the event of the enemy discovering them it will be every man for himself."

In just a few minutes they are safely across the road and are now just ten yards from their target.

The Sergeant whispers, "Come forward Paddy."

He whispers quietly, "Scout round the back and sides and report back." Paddy was ghost like but in missions like this; by far the best man.

Paddy sprinted to the rear of the building, vanished round the side, then he was back signalling all clear.

The Sergeant decided that a direct entry was best. Leading his team across the floor, he ordered, "Twelve pints of your best bitter, barman, if you please!"

You could never be too careful when officers and Redcaps were on the lookout!

# Darkness Falls 3

Darkness falls. Geraldine feels that she has been in bed for hours, checks her bedside clock and realises that it is time to leave.

She looks at her husband, snoring contently beside her and a look of disgust crosses her pretty face. She cannot stop the feeling of loathing that wells up inside her at the sight of her paramour. Twenty years older than her, prematurely bald with a great, flabby gut; how she had grown to loathe him.

Theirs had never been a love match, more a marriage of dynasties. At twenty years old, clinging to her father's arm she had walked down the aisle to wed her forty years old groom. Even then he was losing his hair and the present problem of gross overweight had already begun. He had fallen for her when she was only eighteen and her father had stressed the need for her to 'keep him sweet'. Not to put too fine a point on it her father had claimed that his business would go bankrupt without the friendship.

Undoubtedly he had been kind, showering her with diamonds, emeralds, sapphires, rubies, pearls and gold. In return she gave him two sons who were now eight and six. That side of her marriage was extremely difficult, due to the revulsion she felt for his fat gut. How she hated that thing!

But soon he, and it, would be out of her life for ever.

She rises, pads across the Aubusson carpet to their safe. Quickly she keys in the numbers and waits for the door to open. She begins to carry her jewellery boxes into her dressing room. It requires several trips but at last it is done. She began dropping her best pieces into her Prada handbag. Simon had been emphatic, "Only bring a few pieces to keep them going if his savings did not last." He was so proud, so independent, and so loveable.

She thought of him now, just as she had thought of him one year ago when her husband, Neil, had introduced her to their new butler. With typical 'small man' speech he had growled, "This is Hubert our new butler."

"Simon Sir," the new butler replied in perfectly modulated vowels.

"Whatever," Neil growled in his usual aggressive manner. "Our last butler was called Hubert, so you are Hubert. I pay you and I can call you what I want."

Geraldine was mortified by Neil's bad manners and lack of breeding. A self-made man, it was his proud boast that he could employ lackeys to speak nicely, he was the one who earned the money.

"Of course Sir," replied Simon, "anything you wish. When shall I serve dinner?"

"When I bloody well tell you," growled Neil and walked off. Geraldine silently implored Simon's forgiveness.

Over dinner Neil's bad manners continued, he slouched over the table, licked his knife and complained loudly about the service.

Geraldine was at a loss to explain his behaviour, whispering to Simon that he was not usually like this. As she looked at the two men she could not help but draw unfavourable comparisons. Neil was five feet eight inches, fat, rude, short legged, beetle browed, stubby fingers with broken and chewed nails. She could barely remember the last time he had said please for anything.

Simon was six feet tall with jet black hair. That first night at dinner she had thought he was Clarke Gable or Errol Flynn in Robin Hood. He moved with the feline grace of Nureyev and had the long slender fingers of a concert pianist. Geraldine was certain she fell in love with his hands or maybe it was his long, almost feminine eyelashes. Despite his grace and elegance there was nothing 'sissy' about Simon who oozed masculine charisma.

Was it entirely by accident that his hand had brushed hers as he served dinner and did those deep mahogany eyes look into hers for just a millisecond too long? Whatever the case Geraldine knew she was in love with him before she left the dinner table.

She could feel a flush rise as she imagined making love with him. He would be tender and passionate bringing her to heights she had never achieved with Neil.

Poor Neil, it wasn't his fault that lovemaking was so disappointing. From the beginning all Geraldine had wanted was to get it over as soon as possible. She grew tired of disappointments and sought many ways of avoiding the 'act'.

She is careless in her preparations for flight. Neil had consumed his usual bottle of excellent red wine over the course of the evening and she had doubled his usual sleeping draught to ensure a deep and long night's sleep. From experience she knows he will sleep until noon but then she hears his voice. She creeps over to the bedroom but he is fast asleep, arguing as usual, even as he sleeps.

Geraldine rushes back to her task. The Prada is packed with her favourite 'bits' but more than half of her collection remains in boxes.

With typical self-delusion she tells herself she has earned her little beauties so she fetches another bag.

Without finesse she dumps the entire collection into her second Prada bag, returns the empty boxes to the safe and quietly closes the safe door. She knows Simon will be cross with her for bringing so much but she just can't help herself.

She looks again at her ageing husband. Yes she has earned every last stone. Yes he had been very generous, dressing his wife in a wide array of jewels, pouring twenty million pounds into her father's business to keep it afloat, cruising on the Aegean, the Caribbean and the Mediterranean. Yes he had flown her in a private jet round the world but the truth was she could no longer stand him.

She no longer wanted the mansions, the servants, the Bentley or the Porsche. All she sought was a simple life with Simon. Well, maybe not as simple as Simon wanted. She smiled at the 'simple Simon' but her jewels would prove useful. She smiled again as she heard Simon admonish, "Leave the Bentley, the Porsche, we will be fine in my little run-around." God how she loved that man, his honour, his ethics, he was the most honest man she had ever met. She remembered his honour when she tried to give him a Rolex watch as a Christmas present. She could still hear the hurt in his voice as he reminded her that her husband paid him an excellent salary for the service that he provided. He did not require any gratuities to ensure good service. Geraldine tried to reassure him that it was a gesture to mark the season of goodwill but Simon was firm. He could never afford to buy her such a present so a pair of socks might be more appropriate. He had claimed that he could perhaps buy her a scented handkerchief.

Neil had been off somewhere sailing on his boat and Geraldine dined alone. Most of the staff had the night off as Simon served her meal. She could barely breathe with his closeness, the subtle fragrance of his aftershave, the beauty of his profile and that feline grace.

Geraldine broke all protocol by inviting him to dine with her. Simon's refusal had been charming, seeking to protect her from the barbs of other staff. He whispered, "I think your husband would soon learn of that and he would be likely to misconstrue the situation."

Geraldine loved him all the more. Even now he is thinking of her, protecting her. He adds, "If Madam wishes I could join you for a drink in the salon when the staff have retired for the night."

Madam did wish it and made her preparations. A long leisurely scented bath, an hour spent on her makeup, another hour on deciding what to wear. The final decision was a case of deciding what not to wear.

At midnight she joined Simon in the salon. Over the first cognac she learned how he had worked in the great houses of

England, having trained as a butler with a leading institution. On the second cognacs they were sitting a little too close together, looking too deeply into each other's eyes. The third cognacs were never poured.

Love making on the salon floor with Simon was even better than she could have imagined. Though over quickly it had the promise of more to come and a better tomorrow.

All the tomorrows had been better. They made love at every opportunity, taking risks that normal people would have avoided. Something greater than they drove them into deeper throes of passion.

The affair had been ongoing for just over four months when Geraldine made the momentous decision. Having made love in her own dressing room as Neil snored next door, Geraldine could contain herself no longer, "Let's run away!" she gasped. The sound of her own voice shocked her.

"You could not leave all this," said Simon, "and what about the boys?"

"We could bring them with us," Geraldine cried. Simon looked shocked. "You do not know what you are saying," he suggested. "It is quite likely we will be living in some grubby little apartment. I too love the boys but how could you take them away from here where they have everything? All their lives they have been sheltered, they would be destroyed in a rough council estate. Besides they truly love their father."

Geraldine was downcast. "Yes you are right, they must stay with their father but I am leaving with you."

Simon bowed, "It seems I have no say in the matter."

Geraldine blushed, "I'm sorry, I did not really mean it like that."

"I know," he smiled and plans began.

Tonight is the night. Geraldine has left letters for Neil and the children to explain her decision .She cannot leave without seeing them one last time. She dresses quickly, grabs her travel case and handbags and silently slips into the boys' room.

Both boys are asleep. She bends over, kisses each of them on the forehead and whispers, "Please forgive me but I love him too much."

Not for the first time Simon checks his watch. As usual the bitch is late. He stands by the butler's pantry cursing silently under his breath. Where is she? She was supposed to be here twenty minutes ago. He had turned the burglar alarm off half an hour ago in preparation for flight. He pats his valise for reassurance. Contained therein is a rather fetching Monet and a Matisse which should fetch two million euros on the black market. He had made the switch three months ago for two rather average fakes. As he had expected none of the Philistines had noticed. These were his insurance in the event that Madam changed her mind. It had always been his intention to make off with the jewels. As a connoisseur he had estimated that the selfish bitch had somewhere between fifteen and twenty million euros worth of jewels. While the art was nice, jewels had always been his 'bag' and he knew several crooked 'fences' who would part with five million for the entire haul. Originally he had thought of raiding the safe but then Madam had made herself available to him. This way was much better with no crime involved.

He had gambled that she would be too greedy to leave the jewels behind. In a day or two he would have his savings stolen, at which point she would produce her booty. He would think up some story to justify taking the gems to be valued and perhaps sell one or two pieces. With any luck he could have fenced the gems, sold the art and be in Nice before she even suspected that he was gone.

Impatiently he checked the time once more. No doubt Madam was spending time with those spoiled brats. He smiled at the brilliance of his argument when he had insisted that they stay with their father. He shivers involuntarily at the thought of spending any more time with those hooligans. The idea is too horrendous to countenance. Not once did Simon (if that was his real name) show any concern about abandoning a stony broke woman in Paris, London or anywhere else.

He imagined himself in his yacht in Nice. He estimated that 'his' money should last for two or three years by which time he would have moved on to his next target. There were lots of rich widows and bored wives in the South of France; to a 'grifter' of his ability they would be pushovers.

Geraldine glides across the hall, "Are you there Simon?" she whispers and he steps out from the pantry. He notes with satisfaction that she is carrying two fully stuffed handbags. He draws on fifteen years' experience as a hustler, summons all the sincerity at his disposal and asks, "Are you sure darling?"

She looks at the sweeping staircase, the marble floors and the priceless antiques and whispers, "I'm sure."

He reaches out and takes her hand.

# The Street Lamp

The Street Lamp
'The lamps are going out all over Europe'
Edward Grey
British Home Secretary 1914

14th June 1944
Well, we did see them lit again, but only for twenty five years. Once again the planet is plunged into another World War. For more than four years it seemed that Britain would be overrun by the German Army and Air Force, but now we stand on the brink of success. Or so we are told.

For the past eight days I have watched in trepidation as more than one hundred thousand troops embarked for France. The massive movement goes unabated and already we are hearing of fearsome losses on the beaches of Normandy. Tomorrow it is my turn! Our orders have come through and my group will embark at 0.900 hours.

Tonight my sweetheart and I are meeting for the final time before that fateful day. We embrace under 'our lamp' or more correctly what used to be a lamplight.

Tonight everything is in darkness, though mid- year the heavy clouds have obliterated the moonlight.

We embrace in desperation, perhaps never to see each other again.

How could life be so cruel? We force laughs as we recall other meetings under the lamplight. Here is where we first met on that first date three years ago. I had just commenced work on the South Coast and my darling just happened to be passing as I made my exit from work. We stumbled into each other's arms.

I suppose we were both shy but it is difficult to remain so locked in each other's arms.

We both spluttered apologies for our carelessness and laughed self-consciously.

Even then I knew that this was something special and was certain that I must not let the opportunity slip.

As we were right outside my workplace I suggested we go inside for tea and scones and get over the shock.

Well we got over the shock and arranged to meet by the seashore at what became our lamppost. I suppose others might see it as any old lamppost standing forlornly by the strand. For me though, it was a work of art. Black enamelled metal with scrolled fret work headed by an upturned bowl-like lampshade. The golden glow reflected off my love's face while the shadows danced on the pavement. A trickle of light reflected on the softly murmuring water as I gazed awestruck into the most beautiful blue eyes that I had ever seen.

I cannot tell who moved first, perhaps we were enchanted by the magic of the light but somehow we were in each other's arms.

That was the moment when the artwork became 'our lamplight'. That was the moment we fell in love.

Despite many difficulties our lamppost was our meeting place any time we could get together. Our lamp knew everything about us.

Instinctively I know that our lamppost was sad for us; it knows that it might never see us again as a couple. It knows that I might die in the hell hole that is Normandy.

We did not speak of such things on this last night, we simply clung to each other treasuring every moment.

Then it was time for me to go. I had broken curfew and slipped out without permission, to say goodbye to my lover.

I could hold back no longer, frantically I whisper, "If I should fall tomorrow or over the coming days, come and visit our lamppost. My spirit will be here."

My darling sobs. "If you fall, I will come here on this day each year for the rest of my life."

One last kiss, then I adjust my Red Cross veil, smooth my dress and hurry back to my billet.

N.B. The Red Cross were the first group of females to land in Normandy on 15th June 1944

PPS One female journalist Martha Gellhorn Burk stowed away amongst the 150,000 men landing on D Day

# Fifty Five Years

"Let me ask you, ladies what would happen if the most bubbly, outgoing, optimistic, kind hearted girl was to meet the most dour, dark introverted boy on the planet?"

"No, no ladies, let's imagine that they meet and go out for a dinner date. Imagine that she chitters merrily through the meal as he sits staring in a semi catatonic state. What then?"

"Ladies, I see all of you shaking your heads. I did say this lady was kindness personified! Let's imagine they go for a second date, rambling in the hills. Let's consider that he says, "Hello" when they meet and shakes her hand as they part. How would you behave then?"

"Well she did go on a third date!"

"How do I know? Ladies I was that zombie man. Not only did she go on a third date, she dated me for ten years."

"I can see from your expressions ladies, but no she did not ditch me. I suppose though that, that is what she should have done."

"For ten years she surprised me almost daily, giving me little gifts when it wasn't my birthday or Christmas. Then there were all the times when she invited me to her house for meals."

"No madam, I did not bring wine, flowers, perfume or anything else. I just brought me."

"Madam, you are being sarcastic, of course I thanked her or at least I think I did."

"Ladies you are being impatient! I will tell you what happened after ten years. I did the one surprising thing I ever did in my life (well it surprised me). We were having a meal in a crowded restaurant, the sun was shining in her hair, she was vivacious and I suddenly realised that I loved her."

"No madam, I did not tell her. I dropped to my knees in that crowded restaurant and asked her to marry me. All the other diners cheered and clapped."

"You asked what she said. She said 'yes' immediately followed by 'are you sure?'"

"I was never sure about anything but I brazened it out with a brave 'Yes!'"

"No madam, we did not marry right away, in fact it was five years before that happened."

"Yes, yes, of course you are right, she took the initiative and booked the registry office. She told me she would be there on a certain Saturday and if I still wanted to marry her, I should turn up on the day at eleven am."

"Well I turned up on the day along with forty family members I hardly knew we had."

"We had a lovely reception where she declared to everyone that she was the happiest woman in the world. I just wondered if we had done the right thing."

"She moved into my ramshackle house that night. That was the first time we had spent the night together."

"As you can see ladies, things were different in my day. Pardon? No there was no honeymoon. I had either forgotten to book anything or else I considered it to be a waste of money."

"What is that you asked madam? How long did the marriage last? I find that a little insulting. We were wed forty years ago and we are still together."

"No she is still the same outgoing, bubbly, optimistic, kind hearted person she always was."

"You are absolutely right, madam. It cannot have been easy for her but ever so subtly, ever so gradually she brought about changes. Out went the old clothes, the decrepit furniture, the smoke stained wallpaper, as she worked her miracles."

"No, no I never helped, it was her home now and she could do whatever she wished."

"No madam, I did not do anything around the house. In truth I did not do anything, anywhere. She organised everything, holidays, birthdays etc."

"Why did she stick it?"

"Madam, I do not know, but let me finish with this little story. Last winter we were lying in bed together. We had retired early, because at our age we cannot always afford to heat the house. We got into our pyjamas as quickly as possible and slid into bed. I was lying on my right side when she snuggled up against me for heat. She shivered, snuggled closer and put her left arm around me, as she had done so often in the past, she kissed me on the shoulder and whispered, 'you are the love of my life'."

"You ask madam what I did."

"I turned my head into the pillow so she could not see my joy filled eyes or feel the love in my pride filled heart. And silently I mouthed a prayer to God for giving me the courage to do that surprising thing forty five years ago."

# Dave's Voice

Dave's voice rasps through the air like a wood saw being drawn across a rusty nail. Any hope of quiet contemplation disappears with the arrival of a man who believes his voice should be in constant use.

I think maybe the Irish are all like that, then I remember I too am from the Emerald Isle.

The voice booms out in megaphone force, made worse by the natural amphitheatre in which our villas are built. Dave learned early to speak but, alas, never learned how to listen. Whispering, speaking lowly or slowly is no part of his repertoire.

I seek out the most distant corner of the communal pool but even at twenty metres the voice blasts into my head. The topics are inane and boring. How was your flight? Are you eating out? Which restaurant? Is delivered in decibels that must match the greatest jet aircraft.

I am a quiet man, a solitary sort of individual, content with my own company and my own space.

Dave fails to accept solitariness, insisting I join in, in local activities. I have dined in his company, watched football on television in a local pub, but worst of all I have endured Dave's renditions at Karaoke.

If there is anything worse than listening to Dave talk it is listening to Dave sing. Don't get me wrong, Dave has a very fine singing voice; a rich Irish tenor but I am much too close with no control over the volume.

I try every conceivable device to moderate his speech. I pretend his accent is foreign to my ear, that his speed of speech makes it impossible to grasp every word. Pleas to slow down, tone down and occasionally pause for breath are totally ignored. Ignored with good grace I have to say for Dave is a most personable chap who is helpful in each and every way. He is a devoted father, a loving and faithful husband and perfect in almost every way.

Each summer I pray that our holiday term will not overlap, in order to allow me some time to relax, repair and reflect. I am the sort of person who needs to be alone in order to generate the creative processes that provide my livelihood.

Yet somehow, without prior planning, Dave's voice is the first one I hear on arrival and the last one as he wishes me bon voyage.

Each summer I toy with the idea of selling up and moving elsewhere but I know the fates would somehow contrive against me if I moved. My mind was in such a state that I was certain if I bought a villa in Majorca, his ghost would follow me.

I was lying by the pool cogitating that ten summers with Dave was enough for any man, when he appeared right in front of me. I could barely discern his question, the voice was so low. I could not believe my ears so I asked him to repeat. The voice seemed to come from a very great distance and was soft and melodic, "Would you and your wife like to come round to our house for drinks around eight o'clock this evening?"

I could scarcely believe it, ten years of imploring, of quiet desperation and at last my pleas had worked.

I nodded, dried myself and rushed to my own villa to tell my wife of the miracle of Dave.

When I announced my news, she mouthed something that I couldn't make out so I asked her to speak up.

I could see her mouth moving but I could not hear a single sound. The local doctor referred me to the hospital where the consultant wrote, 'you must not fly'. The remainder of his conversation was with my wife.

Several weeks in hospital, doses of blood thinners, X-rays, MRIs and I'm pronounced fit to go home. I am still profoundly deaf.

Six months have passed in my world of silence. It is summer and we are back in our villa, Dave awaits with concerned expression.

I am fairly certain he is shouting in his usual manner, my wife is laughing and I am cursing myself for all the wasted opportunities when I could have listened to Dave's voice.

# Hi God!

Hi God!

Hi God, how come you never once raised your hand to help me?

Ok, ok, I know I passed my exams at school when I did not deserve to. What about the years I spent in dead end, stinking jobs without hope of escape. Where were you when I was hauling bags of pig meal around the country? And what about those ten stone bags of coals that I lugged around; what about that?

I know, I know, you could argue that it motivated me to attend night school and then go on to university but that was 'me' working hard to escape the gutter.

Yes, I suppose you could have kept me there if you had so wished but my ex-girlfriend did more for me then you did. No doubt you could claim that it was you who put the ideas in her head. That's easy to say but can you prove it?

No, I suppose God does not have to prove anything but it would be nice, if just once or twice you showed me your face.

Did you reach out your hand to help me through my teacher training and my other courses? No, of course you did not. Can you remember the thousands of pounds that I owed when I finished my studies? What help were you then?

Of course, I got well paid jobs and rapid promotions but it took two years to pay back the loans. Character building, I hear you say, or rather I imagine that is what you are thinking?

Some character building when the bank manager threatened to foreclose on my mortgage!

My fault? How was it my fault? Indeed I could have taken a job when I qualified as a teacher but the Dean's offer of a Doctorate was just too good to turn down.

I suppose you will say it was the Dean's fault for giving me the opportunity! Yes I know I had a wife and children who should have been my priority. But, did you warn me of the consequences? I really do not think that one letter from the faculty informing me of yearly fees and a four year duration of study gave a true picture. Of course it is not your fault that I did not consider the cost of books, travel, computers and overseas placements. I did work damned hard during my holidays to earn extra money.

Sorry, sorry, I know I must not swear at you, so why don't you say something?

You are blaming me again because my marriage broke down during the course. Yes I did get too close to my fellow student; it was hardly her fault or mine that my wife did not understand me.

Yes, yes, it is an age old excuse but she really did not understand me.

How could she understand me? I don't know, I did not even understand myself at the time. No I suppose it was me who changed. You ought to know that it is very difficult to go from being a lorry driver to being a PhD student.

You are not on trial here. But could you not have warned me, just this once? I would have listened.

No you are right I would not have listened any more than I would have listened about the hundreds of women over the years.

I suppose women are my weakness. What do you mean only one of my weaknesses?

I know you did not speak. I know it is my guilty conscience or my Super-Ego in Freud speak.

Yes, yes I am showing off and yes I know it is you who is omniscient and omnipotent.

What, surely not all of the seven deadly sins?

Yes I have admitted to you that I have been lustful. No I suppose I did not really care that others could be hurt.

No that is not true; it is not that I did not care, it was just that I never gave it a thought.

Yes God, case proven, I was lustful and insensitive and I probably did hurt others but I too suffered.

I know, I know it is no excuse.

Pride, you can hardly accuse me of pride. I know many people said I was arrogant but that was a cover up for shyness.

Am I sure? Of course I am sure!

Yes, yes I did sign off my letters with a string of fancy donnish letters; but I had earned my PhD, my Masters, my basic degree.

What do you mean I'm at it again? I'm just trying to make a point.

What point? I don't honestly know but you must know, you know all things? I can feel you looking at me and I must protest I have never been vain. I have always thought of myself as being ugly. Who am I trying to kid?

Not you God. You know all things.

Did I boast? Did I brag? Did I manifest false pride?

I suppose I boasted to my family about my achievements and granted I was a master at manifesting false modesty. What do you mean, I'm at it again? Just because I said I was a master!

Ok, ok damned again!

There is no point in talking about envy/ covetousness. I always hated that village where I grew up; a dozen children in two rooms without light or water. And who would want to remain in a house with an outside toilet?!

I worked very hard to escape that misery. How would you feel if you could see rich folk with their big houses, big cars and fancy women?

Oh God, I'm sorry I know you started life in a stable in Bethlehem.

No the 'oh God' is not a swear word, just an ejaculation at my own stupidity.

Would the little bungalow and the old car not have been enough? I suppose it might have been but by then I had met a well-connected widow.

So it was her fault?

Of course not, in fact I have never met a less materialistic person but her whole family were wealthy and upper class.

Am I saying it was her fault that I continued to covet?

No, no, no my pride (of which I have already pleaded guilty) drove me to prove myself to her.

No, of course there is no compunction to prove anything. It is just that the WANTS won't leave me alone. I doubt if I will change now.

So yes guilty of covetousness, guilty of envy.

Am I really guilty of avarice? Am I greedy for possessions and material things?

Of course I have spent a lifetime collecting works of art, fine paintings and sculptures. Can there be harm in that? Yes I own dozens of rare watches and pens that I rarely look at and I have competed (fiercely) at auctions for fine furniture and things of beauty.

Have I ever stolen or cheated to finance my wants? Of course not, I earned it all by the 'sweat of my brow'.

I know you are judging me; maybe not by the 'sweat of my brow' but everything was obtained honestly.

God why are you so harsh? Of course I could have used money to help third world children or others less fortunate than me. In my defence I did sponsor a child in Africa.

I know, I know with the money I spent on indulgences I could have supported an entire village in Ethiopia.

You know God! You do not make life easy!

Yes, yes I know – you do know everything.

I can hardly deny gluttony as I stand here before you four stones over weight and a burden on the state. I won't even bother to make my case I am guilty as charged. Likewise for sloth. I am idle, lazy and disinterested. I like to think that this is a recent thing but in truth all I ever did was just enough to get by. I leaned on family, friends and colleagues at every opportunity. I try to justify my sloth by arguing that I pay for everything that people do for me but we both know I have spent a lifetime of indolence, often to the detriment of people I love.

Oh yes I do love but it has taken until now to realise that love is not enough.

But how can I change the habits of a lifetime?

Why did I leave anger to the last? Probably because I have been filled with blind, unreasoning wrath from the day that I was born.

No of course I cannot know if I was born angry. All I know is that it is the first emotion that I can remember.

All my life I have used that anger to hit out at others and, stupid as it sounds, to punish myself.

No I did not physically strike out but my tongue was a much more effective weapon; used to devastating effect on those I loved best.

Yes God, I am ashamed of it but I am well past forgiveness. You know God, you are one very critical judge. Why would I expect you to listen to me; to help? I'm off now!

Somewhere in the ether God smiled and silently reminded the sinner that He always listened. The problem was that the sinner could not hear.

# I'm Talking to You, God

Oh God, I cry out in anguish why can I not be like others I see around me? Why can't I laugh and run and play in the park, having fun with my friends?

Or why can't I run one hundred metres in less than ten seconds like Usain Bolt; or be a world record holder at five and ten thousand metres like Mo Farah?

Perhaps you could make me a great singer like Placido Domingo or Jose Carreras? Maybe I could be a virtuoso pianist or violinist?

Or I could be a celebrated entrepreneur or billionaire in the Golden Mile in the City?

God, I don't want to be great at everything, to be exceptional at just one thing would be enough.

Look at the talent you gave Pele, Eusebio, Best and Ronaldo, why can't I be like them?

Maybe I could become the new Ghandi, Mother Teresa or Nelson Mandela? I feel I have it in me to be a great humanitarian. Think God, how the world could benefit from my very great talents; if only you would give me some?

My God, I am so frustrated. Look at me, fully mature, without ever having achieved greatness in anything.

Even if you let me be great at some minor sports, I would be eternally grateful. You might let me become a great high jumper, javelin thrower, or a world discus thrower. Any of these would be fulfilling.

Maybe the world could benefit from my great knowledge of microchips or Nano technology if only you would implant this knowledge in my head?

God in his infinite wisdom decided to answer the heart felt plea.

"My son," he said, "You can never be any of these things."

"Why not?" I demand.

God answered, "Because you are a tortoise."

# It's Only a Race

## Gary's Story

Hot favourite to win the National Championships in the 800 metres. I had been two yards ahead entering the final stretch. I was exultant, soon the gold medal would hang from my chest along with automatic entry to the Commonwealth Games and maybe, just maybe the Olympics. The world was my oyster!

In the thirty years that have passed since that day I cannot explain what happened next. Perhaps I slowed down as I anticipated my win, maybe I celebrated too soon. Whatever, in the surge for the line I found myself being overtaken; not once but by three other runners.

The locals and Nationals all proclaimed that I was a spent force and the selectors must have agreed. The gold and silver medallists were both chosen for the Commonwealth Games while I was left to curse fourth place. To pile insult upon injury the Gold medallist, whom I had always previously beaten, went on to win silver in the Games and competed in the Olympics. Subsequently his career soared, making a fortune as an after dinner speaker, television pundit and sitting on prestigious Boards.

Meanwhile I sank into oblivion. I doubt if anyone can remember my glory days on the track. I have never told my wife or my son how close I came to fame.

I spent a further four or five years competing in minor events but the edge was gone. Perhaps it was the bitterness of that 'fourth place' that consumed me. Maybe recourse to alcohol to sustain me or the bitter memories of failure contributed to my decision to retire at twenty-eight years of age without any idea as to how I would earn a living.

The wasted years consumed by self-pity left me broken and pointless. Life had no meaning, I had failed in the only thing that had ever brought me pleasure. I lost myself in Johnny Walker red and later in cheap Scrumpy, finishing up in an Addictions unit at thirty-two years of age.

Physically and mentally I hit rock bottom. A.A. sustained me for a while but I knew that it was only a matter of time before I fell off the wagon.

Then the 'Power greater then myself' dealt me a new hand. She was way out of my league but then so was everyone at that time.

I was sitting at the lakeside, ostensibly feeding the ducks when she joined me on the bench. She must have been sitting for some time as I suffered the shakes with my insides churning and my head crying out for whiskey. Then I became aware that she had spoken but I had to ask her to repeat herself.

"Are you alright?" she reiterated, "You do not look so good."

"I'm OK," I growled then added for some peculiar reason, "just a touch of flu."

Unbelievably she took me to a restaurant, fed me and helped me home to my bedsit. She returned each day until my 'flu' was better. For the first time I really looked at her, she was blondish about five foot six and I guessed around my own age. Her amazing smile lit up the whole room and I was intoxicated by her chatter. I never met anyone who could chatter like her. When I got a 'word in' I asked if she would care to join me for dinner.

It soon became apparent that I had not fooled her for a single moment. "Only if there isn't any alcohol" she responded, adding "my father was an alcoholic and I refuse to become involved with anyone who drinks."

I silently vowed to abstain, a vow I have kept to this day.

Six months later we were married in a small Registry Office with only two witnesses to share our 'great day'. Yes I was at the bottom of the heap but my dear wife supported me through every setback, every 'kick in the teeth' as I struggled to make my way. Two years into our marriage we were blessed with a son and our lives were complete.

We knew from the start that our child was 'gifted'. We marvelled at the creation that we had engendered. By the time our son was ten years old I was in middle management and happy with it. My wife continued in the role as Personal Assistant in a large accountancy firm. Every spare penny was put aside to ensure our son's genius was realised. Kindergarten, Private School and University proved no obstacle to our 'beloved boy'. At twenty years of age he achieved a First Class Honours Degree from a top university and was 'head hunted' by a famous American Institute from which he achieved his doctorate at twenty-three years old.

Much to our surprise and perhaps a little disappointment he refused all offers from several major companies on his return home, choosing instead to join two other friends in something called the new computer age.

At age twenty-five he bought his mother and myself a large Georgian house in a small gated community and suggested that we retire and allow him to take care of us.

To say we were shocked was a master of understatement; the thought of retirement had never entered our heads. After all I had just turned sixty and his mother's 'big' birthday was not due for almost a year.

No we would continue to work and support ourselves. The 'bonny boy' laughed and said, "Dad I know how you worry but I am not going broke. If you wish I will put two million pounds in a bank account for you, to save you from any more stresses at work."

Two million pounds! I almost fainted, how could a boy of twenty-five have two million pounds? The figure was mind blowing.

Nevertheless we declined his offer and continued to work. How could I explain to him the deep insecurities that lurked within me? I had seen 'rock bottom' and it was 'Hell' on earth. I was obsessed by 'that' race and the ignominy of coming fourth. If only I had tried a little harder I could have given my wife and son so much more. I failed to see that my financial input would have been a drop in the ocean to my son. At twenty-six years old he 'bought out' his partners and formed links with Japanese and American entrepreneurs. Together with the Americans and the Japanese he had invented and refined new micro and Nano technology. Almost weekly I read about another new acquisition or invention as he marched worldwide.

Not for a moment did logic enter into my thinking 'I had come fourth in the most important race in my life; I was a failure.' The dark thinking deepened over the years to the point where I was not only a failure, I was unlovable and, in all likelihood, my son was ashamed of me. He travelled the world in private jets, I drove a ten year old Skoda; he consorted with Presidents, I rarely accompanied his mother to the theatre. God, how I wish I had tried harder in that race! My consolation was the fact that I had been blessed by a supportive wife and the most amazing son. I could not ask for better, BUT, the 'internal' critic reminded me that they could have done so much better.

While I took pride in every new achievement by my uber-successful son, I grew gloomier about my own lack of success. No, I was not jealous of his success, but almost daily I wished that I could do something that would make him proud of me. But, of course that was impossible!

When the invitation came I was filled with dread. How could I possibly mingle with the leaders of society, with politicians, nobility and people of the world?

The gold embossed card invited my wife and me to the Businessman of the Year awards where our son was going to be honoured. We debated for hours but at last agreed that we must attend.

I will not attempt to describe the luxury of the surroundings nor the banquet which was provided. I can only say that I could scarcely eat a bite as I was overcome with nerves.

The presentation was led by the Lord Mayor who introduced our son as the fourth richest man in Britain. He joked about the fact that the richest man, a steel magnate was approaching ninety years old, the second, a wealthy Duke had inherited his money while the third richest was descended from a two hundred year old dynasty. The Mayor concluded by saying that ten billion pounds at the age of thirty was a pretty good achievement!

Amidst the laughter and cheers our son was invited on to the stage to accept his 'Businessman of the Year' award.

My wife and I agreed that it was the only time that we had seen our son display nervousness. His voice shook slightly as he accepted his award, then he added, "I wish to thank two very special people, without whom this award would have been impossible." He went on to say how we had scrimped and saved to provide the best for him and his voice shook as he said, "Dad, Mum, I cannot begin to tell you how proud I am of you and how much I love you." Through my tears I was vaguely aware of the entire audience rising to their feet and then the applause began as they saluted us.

Words cannot describe how much I loved my son at that moment.

When silence was restored our son laughed and ended his speech by saying, "It's not a race you know and fourth is not a bad place to be."

The audience erupted. I reflected, "It was a race and fourth was not such a bad place after all."

# JG. A Working Class Hero.

## (is something to be)

### John Lennon

J.G. stared intently at the page that lay before him. A shudder, part elation and part deep unspoken anger, coursed through him. He could feel the tension build within as his body stiffened, his hands became fists and his narrowed eyes took in the scene.

The Palladian manor was not as large as some of the houses he had visited, the twenty thousand acres less than half the size of some others. Despite the 'drawbacks' the Italian styling spoke of class, elegance and long tradition. The 'acres' had everything a man could want, arable land, two lakes, bubbling streams, afforestation all set in an area of outstanding natural beauty.

Over the previous six months he had scoured the 'Net', travelled the length and breadth of the country searching for his utopia. He had seen places of history, of great beauty, of ideal location but nothing moved him as the present scene touched him.

He had chanced upon the property almost by accident. Idly toying with his computer as he breakfasted in his London study, his interest was immediately captured as the estate filled the screen.

This estate was very different to another estate he had known as a boy. That estate had been rough, run down, with violence simmering just below the surface. Violence not just on the outside but inside in his fear filled home. A violent father, a terrified mother, half -starved children and pariahs from other 'nicer' families in their village. Hate came early and easily to him. A quiet child he easily became the focus of his father's uncontrollable rages. By the time he ran away from home at fifteen years old he knew only fear and hatred. No one had spoken to him on that day more than twenty five years ago, when he fled. His only thought as he left the house was that one day he would return and avenge himself against his tyrant father and the villagers who had alienated, abused and insulted him.

He shook himself free from his reverie as he had sought further information about this estate. The asking price was ten million pounds for the ten bedroomed, six reception etc. He had smiled to himself at the price; a mansion and twenty thousand acres for the price of a three bedroomed terrace house in the Capital: And his house had many more bedrooms than that.

His call to the estate agent was picked up at the first ring, when he offered the asking price.

At first the agent was sceptical, no one spent ten million pounds without seeing what they were buying. It was only when he provided details of his present address and businesses that the agent allowed the excitement of a hefty commission to grow in his heart. The only condition that he had placed upon the purchase was the need for immediate possession.

The agent became increasingly oleaginous, "Sir with the kind of money that you have I would go over and evict the owners myself. Fortunately the house is unoccupied so I cannot envisage any problems." Finally the agent had sought clarification of the buyer's intent regarding the estate houses and the village that was part of the estate.

J.G. mused for some moments before declaring that he was not yet decided on his course of action in that direction. Somewhat maliciously he had mentioned that he might demolish the village and create another fish stocked lake for his own pleasure. J.G. was fairly certain that this line of thought would soon make its way back to the people of the village.

Now he was standing by the gates of his newest property. He could just discern the house at the top of the long winding, rhododendron lined avenue. He eased the Maserati along his new driveway, up the gentle incline and then he was standing outside his new home. He experienced a glow of satisfaction as he took in his new surroundings. He walked across the shingle pathway and gazed down the valley towards the village that he had once known so well. From his vantage point he could just detect the chimney of his old two up, two down home with its outside toilet and it's inside hell. As his eyes began to scan his village his thoughts were interrupted by a polite cough and a gentle, "Sir." When he turned it took all of J.G's iron will to prevent himself from recoiling in shock and horror. The middle aged man who introduced himself as butler and head of the household was the same school prefect who had made J.G's life hell during the final three years of his schooling. J.G. fixed a smile on his face and made a mental note to fire the butler immediately. He realised the butler was speaking, "The staff are gathered in the reception hall to meet you, Sir."

J.G. wondered what further shocks awaited. Firstly he met the indoor staff, recognising only one of them. One of the maids was the little girl who used to smile at him at school and occasionally share her lunch with him. Her job was safe! Then it was the turn of the outdoor staff. Standing facing him were two brothers whom he hated more than any others in the world. These two had bullied, mocked and made his life miserable throughout his school years. One was farm manager, the other a farm labourer, both lived in tied cottages on the estate. Tomorrow they would get their letters of dismissal and notice of eviction. He thought it strange how he remembered them so vividly when they did not recognise him. Well, perhaps not so strange, the ragamuffin boy of fifteen had become a forty year old millionaire who oozed wealth and power from head to feet. His hair was styled by one of

London's leading hairdressers, a twenty thousand pound Rolex rested on his left wrist and he wore the finest John Lobb shoes upon his feet. Though casually dressed it was obvious that the jacket and trousers were Savile Row, the shirt Jermyn Street and of course there was the Maserati outside. Right now J.G. wished he had brought the 'Rolls'.

His perfectly modulated tones conveyed a merciless message. His requirements were simple, he did not need a large staff. "I have no doubt that your previous employer will give you excellent references and I shall honour your salary in lieu of one month's notice. Regrettably I will need the keys of your accommodation by the end of the week." He turned to the housekeeper and the girl from school, "Apart from you ladies, I will not require any other staff." He made no attempt at friendliness, "That is all, good night."

Unaccompanied he familiarised himself with his new home and settled upon the bedroom that would be 'his'. Then he returned to the drawing room. Firstly, he spread out the map of the village and the ledger containing the names of his tenants. With a thin smile he realised that more than half of the villagers were the same people who looked down on him all those years ago. Well who was looking down now?

Again he scrolled through the names of all the people in the eighty houses that now belonged to him. Decisions always came easy but now he wondered if he should quadruple the rents or simply evict the lot of them? Still undecided he checked his remaining possessions within the village; church, school, library, village hall, sports fields and duck pond. What to do? What to do?

In his mind's eye he saw the frightened boy denied access to the cricket and football pitches and too dirty to sit in the library. Well he was not dirty now!

He retraced that fearful flight from the horror that was his life. He recalled the weeks of wandering, then his rescue by the army recruiting sergeant. Two years boys' service, then commissioned as a second lieutenant into an infantry regiment. Eight years of active service followed, then fast tracked promotion and he left the services as a major at twenty five.

Four years at university, economics degree in hand he commenced in the City. Then striking out on his own he was a millionaire at thirty five, followed by five years of unparalleled success. Success came easy as he sharpened his ruthless streak that had been so useful during his army career. It mattered not a jot to him who lost as long as he won. Friends never entered his life and a short lived marriage only served to enhance his cynicism. Single and a couple of million pounds lighter he resolved never to allow emotions to affect any part of his life. His only regret was that he could not exact revenge on his long dead father nor did he consider erecting a headstone for his pathetic mother.

A more 'rounded' man would not have taken so much pleasure in the removal of the staff from the estate. He was particularly pleased with the expression on the now ex-butler's face as he handed over his keys. J.G. made no attempt at conversation nor offered good wishes as his old tormentor trudged down the driveway to catch a bus.

Having cleared out the estate servants, it was now the turn of the villagers. A meeting arranged for the village hall was packed to capacity. J.G. strode in, announced his intentions to quadruple the rents and left before protests could begin. Some long remembered slights and hurts were rectified by serving eviction notices on his former enemies.

Then he decided to visit the school. Why not, he thought after all he owned the place. Without care nor consideration he arrived at the school unannounced. He walked straight into the secretary's office and demanded to see the principal. When the principal arrived J.G. was delighted to see she was accompanied by her vice principal, 'well, well!' he thought, Miss Delaney principal and Master Rogan vice principal, two of the most evil scumbags who ever lived. He could still hear the swish of their canes, the crashing impact with his fingers and the searing pain. Imagine that, he thought, somebody promoted these brutes! The thin smile reappears, no doubt now, he would close this dump down. Miss Delaney flounces into her office demanding an explanation for her removal from class. She glares at J.G. and demands, "What can I do for you?"

"Not so much what you can do for me, but more what can I do for this building?" he responds.

"What do you mean, what you will do with the school?" the Principal asks, "Who are you?"

"Actually, I own this building," J.G. responds, "in fact I own the entire village having bought the estate."

Instantly Miss Delaney transmogrifies into a creeping sycophant. "How delightful, you must meet the pupils."

Like a tornado he is whisked round the school. He has to admit, despite his feelings about the Principal, that the school seems well run if somewhat small.

The reception class was all a buzz as were those classes that used to be called P1 and P2. Then they moved to P3. J.G. said, "This where you taught Miss Delaney do you still teach this class?" "Indeed I do," she responded, "I am very proud of the discipline that I introduce at this stage." "Are you?" J.G. asked as he glanced around the almost silent class. "How did you know that I teach P3?" Miss Delaney asked J.G.

"Because that is where I first met you," J.G. replied, "it is where you did your best to ruin my life."

Miss Delaney's shock registered as she blanched visibly. "I have never set eyes on you before today," she protests. "That is probably true," J.G. responds, "you could not bear to look at the ragbag at the back of the class. Remember Smelly get to the back of the class! Remember you are good for nothing but jail, remember Miss Delaney?" Miss Delaney had come over quite faint. "Why are you saying this?" she asks, "I do not know you, I think it is time you left," her voice was small.

"No, Miss Delaney, it is you who are leaving and everyone else in this hell hole."

Just then J.G. found his eyes drawn to the rear of the room where that horrible woman had confined him for an entire year. Sitting there on 'his' chair was another ragamuffin, anger blazing from his eyes. J.G. knew exactly how that boy felt as he had felt it for more than thirty years. As he approached, the boy adopted the same defensive position, the same defensive tone that J.G. had assumed for most of his life.

J.G. looked intently at the child seeing a replica of a younger self. Almost forty years of pain welled up within him, tears flowed unheeded as he reached out to take the boy's hand. The child cowered before him. "It's all right son, I am here to help you. Why are you sitting here?" The boy's voice was shrill, angst filled, "That bitch hates me. She picks on me because we are poor!" God J.G. thought, she is still doing it after thirty years. Not for the first time he wondered how such people could be teachers. Did they not know the powerful negative effect they had on children? J.G. could not hold back any longer, forty years of hate and fear erupted in great bursts of sobbing.

The poor emaciated child reached out and took his hand, "Are you all right Mister?" he asked in a worry filled voice.

"I am now," J.G. replied. "How often do you sit here?" J.G. asked.

"Every day!" the boy responded.

"Well no longer," J.G. exclaimed, "where do you live?" To his shock and horror he discovers that the boy and his mother live in his old house. "Right," J.G. said, "Let's go and find your mother." Outside the end terrace, J.G. shivers involuntarily, surely he could not let the hell of this house harm another child.

The lady who answers the door is just as emaciated as her son. J.G. says, "I have brought your son home, I would like to help."

The inside of the house is spartan but spotlessly clean. J.G. asks, "Just you and the boy live here?"

"Yes," she said, "my husband left last year. We have no money and we cannot pay off the debts accrued by his drinking." J.G. explained that he had once lived in this house and it had left him with hate filled memories. He added, "That it had taken just one look in her son's eyes to begin restoration."

"Madam," he asked, "would you accept a job in my house where you and your son can live in the butler's apartment? Perhaps your son and I can rescue each other!"

# Loves Farewell

I found her lying there, half in, and half out of the kitchen. I'd left her only minutes before resting in the sun trap in the back garden.

She was barely conscious as I lifted her and carried her inside. Gently I laid her down on the bed that I'd made for her in the living room.

Blood flecked saliva seeped from her mouth, a mouth that lay open and dribbling. Eyes that had once been so vital and animated now seemed pain racked and despairing. Silently her eyes scanned mine, imploring me. But imploring me for what? Was she trying to tell me to end her suffering or something else? I knew not what. I patted her head as I had done so often in the past, assuring her that everything would be alright. But everything was not alright and we both knew it.

My reverie is interrupted by a call from the back garden. "Are ye in Jamie?" the voice is rich, lilting and filled with concern.

"Aye, I'm in Jock," I respond, "We're in the living room."

Jock has been my nearest neighbour since we came to this hill farm several years ago. He is large and awkward with words but has a heart made of pure gold but Sheila shows no sign of recognition.

"Things look bad," he added.

"Aye," I say, "she normally gives you a great welcome."

"She does that," Jock asserts, "none better."

He gazes down at a lifeless Sheila. "No" he adds, "not like her at all."

These are more words than Jock has spoken for days. High hill farmers are not noted for wordiness and now is no different.

Apart from the 'bob' of his throat one would have been hard pressed to discern his emotion. But I know exactly how he feels. The big ham fisted hand reaches down, ruffles the back of Sheila's head and whispers, "Goodbye, old girl."

I imagine he is feeling the same emotions as myself, sharing the same pain. Memories flood in of Jock and his collie and Sheila and me out on the hills in all weathers tending our flocks. I'm sure he remembered the annual event of bringing the flocks down the mountain for their annual health check and sales. How Sheila and I had hurrahed across the hilltops, totally at one with nature.

The years have flown and Sheila has finished her last round up; of that I am certain.

I have watched with growing despair as the evil cancer has eaten into her soul.

The eyes are looking at me again, pleading. I can almost hear it but still I cannot be sure what she is asking. I stroke her head. I try unsuccessfully to dribble some water into her mouth. I retrieve ice cubes and touch them to her lips. There is no response.

I cannot watch this suffering any longer. I unlock the cabinet, take out the rifle and insert one bullet into the magazine.

I press the trigger and the suffering ends for my darling wife.

# Mary Coughed 1

Mary coughed discretely and slipped the folded note into the President's hand.

All eyes are upon him as he unfolds the paper and frowns.

Every heart around the table beats faster: The Homeland Security people pray that no bombs have been detonated in any major city. Silently they think Washington, New York, Los Angeles, San Francisco and consider the odds against each being a target.

The Secretary of State 'runs through' the trouble spots of the world; Ukraine, Russia, Syria, Iraq, Afghanistan, Sudan, Israel and Gaza, Israel and Palestine, Israel and Iran and Pakistan. She thinks of the price the country pays to police the world.

Several Secret Service men pray that none of their agents have been detected while the money men worry about added costs to the existing trillion dollar debts.

All this is conveyed by one frown from the President. He again examines the note; Armed forces Chiefs pray that they have enough men at the ready, to fly to the latest trouble spot.

It's been a long hard day for the President. A breakfast meeting at seven a.m. to discuss an attack upon a school in North Carolina. A television interview to address the nation and condolences offered to parents whose children had been slain by one twisted loner with a machine gun and several pistols.

Mid-morning he had had a meeting with the anti-rifle lobby, then a meeting with the Israeli Ambassador. Apart from coffee he had not eaten since rising at six o'clock in the morning.

The afternoon meeting of the emergency council had gone on much longer than expected. Caterers had provided canapés and other nibbles that had gone largely untouched.

It was this meeting that Mary had interrupted, an occasion that was almost unprecedented. Every member round the table was on tenterhooks. What catastrophe had befallen the world? The unspoken questions reverberated around the room. Had Russia launched a nuclear attack? Had North Korea invaded its southern neighbour?

Everyone knew Israel had the 'bomb'. Had she nuked Iran back into the eighteenth century? And still the moneymen fretted at potential cost.

The President re-opened the slip, frowned again and looked round for Mary.

Mary had left the room.

The President stood up followed by everyone round the table.

"Sit down, ladies and gentlemen. I have to leave you for fifteen minutes or so. Something has just come up but please help yourselves to coffee and cake until I return."

The President rolled the slip of paper into a ball and threw it into his waste paper basket, then turned and left the room.

The White House Chief of Staff rummaged among the litter and retrieved the slip of paper. He smoothed out the paper and immediately recognised the First Lady's distinctive style. The note was short and to the point.

"I have just had a long and scented bath. I am reclining on our bed, wearing the black, see-through negligee that you bought. I have nothing on underneath. Can you afford to wait?"

The Chief of Staff slipped the note into his pocket, smiled and joined his colleagues for coffee!

# Mary Coughed 2

Mary coughed, hoping to draw the President's attention as she crossed the room. Silently she placed a folded paper by his side and left.

Angrily, the President threw the paper on a heap of others sitting before him. How many times had he told her not to interrupt him when he was at a meeting? He silently tut-tutted to himself, scribbling a note to reprimand Mary when the meeting concluded.

There was something about Personal Assistants that made them think they held the reins; yes he would definitely have a word with her when this was over.

What made things worse was the fact that she had interrupted at a critical moment. For several hours they had discussed the financial implications of their plan; arguments had ebbed and flowed, often in meaningless circles. He had just begun to feel that the major decision could be reached, when Mary interrupted the proceedings. In those few seconds the doves and hawks had regrouped, enabling them to further develop their arguments.

The President sighed, remembering how he had canvassed for nomination of the highest office of all. It had not been easy, with glad handing, back slapping, expensive dinners and cogent arguments. How proud he had been when the results were announced, imagining a glorious road forward. His wife had thrown her arms around him, kissing him in full view of the other delegates. He hadn't known whether to be proud or embarrassed, perhaps a little of both.

Having held office for two years, he was beginning to have his doubts. Despite having been involved for many years he had little knowledge of the back biting, the gossiping and penny pinching at the very top.

He was heartily sick of the grey men in grey suits who constantly reminded him of the need to balance the books. He had been elected on a wave of euphoria; catching the mood for social reform. He had argued at many forums for the overwhelming need to improve the lot of children and young people. They were the future and that was where money needed to be spent.

His backers had nodded sagely, pointing to the fact that he was young (ish), energetic and with experience of the real world.

Yet, here he was two years on, worn out with the arguments and tight purse strings. He had finally decided that he would not run for re-election; he was just too tired, two years in power had aged him beyond belief.

With an effort he snaps out of his reverie, calls the meeting to order and invites further comments.

He drifts in and out of awareness. Words like balance sheets, cost benefit analysis, efficiency and effectiveness leave him cold. He worries that he will become like them; the grey men.

He looks at his watch for the umpteenth time as the arguments flow around him.

He is just about to bring the meeting to a close when Mary re-enters the room. Another cough, another slip of paper and she is gone.

Idly he unfolds the paper. "Your dinner is ruined. What sort of idiots need five hours to appoint a part time grounds man to cut the grass on a non- league football pitch?"

He groans, closes the meeting and decides to buy fish and chips on the way home!

# Mary Coughed 3

Mary coughed as the chill night air tickled her throat. She shivered involuntarily and John took his woolly scarf and wrapped it round her. He pulled her coat tightly around her and kissed her gently on the cheek.

John loved the feel of her skin against his lips. If truth be told he loved everything about her.

"Don't worry," he murmured, "we're almost there."

"Almost where?" she asked.

John laughed secretively. "You'll know when we get there."

He had been planning this night for the past three months. Everything had to be perfect to reflect the perfect love they shared.

Two years ago tonight, they first met. A song from South Pacific leapt into his head, "Some enchanted evening – across a crowded room." That was how it had been; he had been standing with his mates when he glanced at the mirror behind the bar. Even the reflection was a hammer blow to his heart as she smiled displaying her small perfect teeth.

He had turned around and there she was, 'eyes meeting eyes' across a crowded bar.

He vaguely recalled someone saying that it took weeks or months to 'fall in love'; he was in love before they had even spoken.

Life took on a new meaning, the skies were bluer, the sun shone more brightly and the stars sparkled just for her. They went everywhere together, did everything together, often sharing the same thought.

The long hours of separation, as each laboured at their jobs served only to enhance the daily joy of reunion at the end of the day.

He was somewhat surprised that she had forgotten that this was their anniversary but that only made this evening even better. He could hardly wait to see the look on her face when he sprang his surprise.

Nothing had been left to chance. He listened intently to her friends as they described her ideal engagement ring. He made countless drawings on his laptop always checking with her nearest and dearest and always swearing them to secrecy.

The perfect ring had cost rather more than he had hoped but she was worth it and more.

At present it nestled in a box in his jacket pocket. He touched the pocket to reassure himself that it was still there.

Then they were in the Michelin starred restaurant and seated at the best seats in the house. The quartet that he had hired played softly in the background.

A subtle scent from the candles perfumed the air around their table. Two red roses formed the centrepiece of the small floral arrangement on their table.

The waiter takes her coat and his scarf, offers the menu and the wine list and invites them to order pre dinner drinks. A magnum of champagne is chilling in its ice bucket just out of Mary's sight.

Each course is better than its predecessor but he barely tastes it in expectation of what is to come.

He reminds her of the date and a tear forms in her eyes. He can barely contain his excitement, she is overcome with emotion and has obviously guessed his intent.

He drops on one knee, withdraws the precious package from his pocket and pops open the clasp exposing the sparkling diamond. Breathlessly he says,

"I love you, Mary, will you marry me?"

Her answer is almost inaudible,
"I've met someone else."
In the background the band strikes up Con-grat-u-lations!

# Mary Coughed 4

Mary coughed. David immediately clamped a hand across her mouth but he knew it was too late. They had dashed to the safe room as soon as they became aware of the Hostiles.

David had spent most of last winter digging beneath the floor of their adobe building, removing hundreds of tons of soil, stones and shale. He was proud of the final result, feeling certain that his cellar could not be detected from above. Mary had praised him regarding his ingenuity; as they descended into the cellar. Several strong fibres could be pulled, drawing the old rug above into place.

They had been in the cellar for fifteen minutes when the first hostile entered the house. The temperature upstairs in their New Mexico home was over 100 degrees Fahrenheit and David guessed it was fifteen to twenty degrees higher in the safe room. The air was stale, burning their lungs with the effort to breathe.

They could clearly hear the step of bare feet on the wooden floor above. David signalled to Jack that he must keep still and very quiet. Jack was only three but he knew not to make a sound when the Apaches were near. Dad had warned him that the Apaches were at war with the Yankees and the Mexicans and would kill him on sight. Jack had no idea what Yankees or Mexicans were but it sounded fearful to him.

It was so boring in the safe room and he wished that Daddy would play some of his favourite games. Daddy seemed more preoccupied with his rifle and handgun and Jack knew that 1882 was a dangerous time to be in America.

The room was like a furnace, the air grew hotter and hotter and breathing was becoming impossible. Then Mary coughed.

All movement above stopped, then someone lowered himself on to the floor. Downstairs all three stood stock still. David raised his rifle aiming it directly at Jack. They had long since decided that they would never let themselves be taken. David held a bead on Jack for several long seconds then despairingly lowered the weapon. He could not bring himself to harm his beloved child.

Should they fight it out, should they start firing through the floorboards? Interminable seconds passed then the lid was opened.

He could have killed three or four of the hostiles but David had never killed anyone or anything in his entire life. One of the hostile's gestured and David lay down his rifle.

Rough hands pulled them upstairs and into the open. A hunting party of twenty or more hostiles sat mounted on their coloured ponies.

David and Mary 'took in' the scene, clinging desperately to each other, with Jack pressed into his mother's skirt. They knew instantly who the leader of the tribe was; though dressed almost exactly like the others one man exuded power as hatred glittered from his eyes.

David's only hope was that all would be killed quickly and Mary would not be taken as a slave.

The leader raised his spear and twenty bowmen took aim.

As the leader raised his spear the sun reflected brilliantly off the metal, creating light images in all the colours of the rainbow.

Jack broke free and ran to the Chief. Showing no sign of fear, Jack's childish voice rang out, "Nice man play with Jack."

For a moment the hatred vanished from the mighty Chief's eyes as he reached down and patted Jack's golden curls.

Mary launched herself forward but was restrained by two muscular warriors. Mary cried out in desperation. "Don't hurt him, take him but do not harm him."

The Chief summoned one of the warriors forward. His voice was hard, uncompromising, obviously accustomed to total obedience.

The warrior spoke respectfully to his Chief. A look of puzzlement crossed his face, again he spoke to the warrior.

The warrior spoke directly to Mary in almost perfect English.

"You would give up your son to save his life?"

Mary's answer was instantaneous, "I would give anything to save my son." Beside her David nodded.

With a graceful bound the Chief dismounted and placed his hands on Jack's shoulders. He barked to his interpreter who relayed his words.

"I am Goyathly, Chief of the Chiricahua Apache. White men call me Geronimo. White men murdered my wife and three children. White men have sought to remove the Apache from the face of the earth."

The name Geronimo struck deep into David's soul. Here was the most feared Indian in all of the Southern States, he was known to be merciless.

David took a step forward. "I have never killed any living thing. I am a pacifist who cherishes life." The warrior conveyed David's words.

Geronimo spat out "Pah," pointed to the hens clucking around the house and said, "You kill hens," in perfect English.

"I do not," declared David, "we raise them for their eggs and nurture them for all of their lives."

Geronimo knelt beside Jack, pointed and demanded, "You eat hens?"

"Of course not," the piping voice seemed to fill the valley.

David spoke once more, "I have a Government paper that shows that I bought this land."

Geronimo growled, "We have many papers from your Government, all worthless!"

Mary coughed again.

David swept his arm around, "We grow maize, potatoes, tomatoes, squash, pumpkins and we keep these hens. To us life is sacred. Take what you will!"

Mary's cough had got worse.

Geronimo took a pouch from his belt, a warrior brought water. Some leaves from the pouch were mixed with the water and brought to Mary.

"Drink," Geronimo commanded.

Fearful of her life Mary obeyed, swallowing the foul mixture. Immediately her pain eased. Geronimo took Jack's hand and together they walked around the garden. He tore several different herbs and threw them to Mary, pointing to her throat.

David and Mary felt the tension leave the air. Then Geronimo drew his knife, held Jack's hand and made an incision in his thumb. Geronimo did the same to his own thumb then allowed the blood to mingle.

"Blood brothers," he announced, "as long as Geronimo lives you live be safe here."

Mary collapsed to her knees. David did his best to support her though his legs had also turned to jelly.

In a single bound Geronimo remounted. He reaches down, pats Jack's head, grasps his hand and swings him up behind him.

Geronimo turns his pony and the tribe ride south.

# Mary Coughed 5

Mary coughed. He obviously hadn't heard her so she coughed again, louder this time. He spun round in his seat until he was directly facing her.

More handsome than Paul Newman, more beautiful than Pierce Brosnan, more masculine than Steve McQueen: Six feet of sheer temptation sitting on a bar stool and he was all hers.

"Would you like to dance?" Mary asked.

A look of horror crossed his face as he looked across to the area for dancing. "All the money in the world would not persuade me to go on that floor" he replied.

Mary could feel the colour spreading up her neck and into her face. "You cannot refuse me it's a ladies choice," she said.

The poor victim was speechless.

"Surely I'm not that ugly?" Mary added.

"No, no," he answered "it is not just that I have two left feet, I am petrified, and I simply can't dance."

"Everybody can dance," Mary claimed wondering how she could retrieve herself from the embarrassing fiasco.

"We could just walk round the floor."

He looked across at what he thought was jiving. "I'm sorry," he said "I'm totally uncoordinated."

Mary realised from the tone of his voice that he felt the same desperation that had engulfed her. A quote from her old professor sprang to mind, "Those whom the Gods' favour they cause also to suffer." She wasn't sure if she was applying the quote to him or herself.

Mary 'came clean'. She nodded across the room, "My friends saw you and dared me to ask you for a dance. Do you mind if I sit with you for a minute or two otherwise my friends will ensure my life is not worth living?"

He stood, extended his hand and said, "My name is Brian and we cannot put your life at risk. Do sit down. Would you like a drink?"

Mary blushed scarlet, sat down and asked if she might have a cocktail.

Brian summoned the waiter, ordered something exotic and suggested that she tell him her name.

"Mary," she mumbled, clearly embarrassed. She scrutinised him surreptitiously (or so she thought). He was clearly a man of some wealth and status. Mary decided the well-cut suit would have cost more than two thousand pounds, she noted the Cartier watch, the John Lobb shoes, the designer belt and the shirt probably from Jermyn Street. Despite the obvious wealth he seemed totally unaffected.

Despite priding herself on being a great listener Mary learned nothing about Brian other than that he was in business. He did not volunteer what that business was.

Mary surmised that his business must be flourishing. Surprisingly Mary found herself pouring out the story of her life. Her school days in the 'sticks', University at Cambridge, coming to London and her work in the banking sector (this piece of information she volunteered with a laugh and an apology).

She found herself telling him about her ambitions, her failed relationships, nudging thirty and single for the previous eight months.

Mary almost jumped when the barman, discretely, called last orders.

With a start she realised that they had been talking for three hours and to her horror, she realised that she had imbibed at least six or seven cocktails at Brian's expense.

"Oh my God!" she gasped, "I will have to go." The words poured from her, "Where are you staying? Will you be back next week? Perhaps I can pay for the drinks next time?"

Brian laughed, "In order, I am staying here, no I will not be here next week but perhaps the following one and no you don't need to buy drinks for me."

Mary begged one last favour, "Would you walk me to the door?"

Brian laughed again, "I know, for your friend's sake!"

But that was only partly true.

As fate would have it Brian was not back for five weeks. He was not to know that Mary had been back to the hotel every Friday night in the off chance that he would be there. Despite several offers she always went home alone.

He was sitting on the same bar stool when Mary coughed. "Like to dance?" she asked.

Brian smiled, "And ruin my good John Lobb shoes, I saw you looking at them?"

It was Mary's turn to smile, "Let me buy you a drink, after all it is my turn?"

Over the course of the evening and several drinks, Brian explained his hectic lifestyle. With offices in London, Paris and New York he lived the life of a gypsy making it difficult to form lasting relationships.

Mary laughed, "I didn't ask for a relationship, only for a dance!"

Brian returned her laugh, "Yes, one of the things I cannot give you!"

Mary reminds him that she did not ask him to give her anything.

The verbal sparring, the laughing and the cocktails lasted until closing time. This time he did not need to be asked to escort her to the door. He hailed a taxi, kissed her on the cheek and assured her he would be back in the hotel in one week.

The days dragged and then it was time to return to the hotel. Mary stayed in the hotel that night and several more nights over several months. If their relationship was limited by his frenetic work rate, she was willing to make the sacrifice.

There were nights as she sat alone in her room that she wished for more but in the future they would have more time together. This frenetic lifestyle would not last forever.

As their relationship strengthened and deepened they did manage to get some extra hours together, occasionally driving to Cambridge or dining in little bars by the Thames.

Today was such a day. The sun was high in the sky, a soft breeze was blowing along the river as swans elegantly glide past.

They are sitting at a secluded table by the river when a child's voice rings out, "Daddy, Daddy," and the boy runs towards Brian.

Mary sits in shocked silence as Brian stands and moves towards the boy. He sweeps him up in his arms and showers kisses on the boy's head and face.

An elegantly dressed, beautiful woman looks at Brian and softly murmurs, "We flew over to give you a surprise but it seems it is a day of surprises for everybody."

Mary felt hot tears well up in her eyes, involuntarily she coughed.

# Mary Coughed 6

Mary coughed. Daddy and Mummy stood over her, stroking her head.

Over and over they muttered, "It will be alright darling" but deep down they knew it would not be alright.

They looked at her poor wasted body as she fought for breath. How could this happen, after all she was only eleven years old?

The disease had struck out of the blue, now six months later their little darling is fighting for every breath. The nurse tests her temperature, her blood pressure, adjusts the intravenous fluid that is providing the only sustenance that Mary can tolerate.

The nurse completes her examination. There is no need to ask, the nurse's expression says it all. Daddy wordlessly begs with his eyes but the nurse cannot keep eye contact. Her gaze falls to the floor and she moves to leave the room. Mummy places her hand lightly on the nurse's arm.

"Is she in pain?" she asks.

"No," the nurse answers truthfully "there is a strong analgesic added to the I/V infusion."

"Can she hear us?" Mummy asks.

"I am sorry but I cannot tell," the nurse's response is a mere whisper.

Daddy strokes the back of Mary's head. "How long?" he asks.

"Not long," the nurse responds "but better you ask the consultant when he arrives."

"Yes, yes of course," Daddy mutters to no one in particular. Mummy takes the large, hard-working hands in hers. They cling to each other in their shared misery.

Daddy starts reminiscing with his beloved Mary. Mummy whispers, "She cannot hear you," but Daddy keeps on talking. "Do you remember the day we all went to the beach? you were the centre of attention, so beautiful everyone getting their photographs taken with you? And can you remember when we went to stay on Pappy's farm?" There was a sob in Daddy's voice, "Remember the fun you had with Pappy's collies? Remember your disgust when the Labrador licked your face?"

Mary coughed and a trickle of blood speckled saliva fell from her lips. Mummy reached down and removed the blood. Mary's breathing was becoming more distressed so Mummy rang for the nurse.

More observations were made. The nurse whispers, "Not long now."

Daddy cried, "Not yet, there are so many stories to remind her about, so many memories to help her in to the next life."

Mummy's tears were flowing freely while Dad's breath escaped in hacking sobs.

Mary's cough got weaker.

"It's time," the soft voice whispered. The vet prepares his instruments and soon Mary is gently put to sleep.

# Old George

George could not be certain when it was that he became 'old' George

At the time of his last divorce, aged seventy, ex-wife number three referred to him as Grumpy George.

Despite protests from the defence barrister the judge allowed the term 'grumpy' throughout the hearing, almost certainly determining the outcome.

George was glad to be rid of the old harpy, but how could he be thought of as grumpy? Why, he remembered vividly smiling at his son's christening.

Somewhere along the way Grumpy George became Old George; probably when he began talking out loud to himself.

He would remind himself he was hungry; "Right George, time for breakfast." And, every week or so he would say, "Ok George it's bath day." George put it all down to loneliness and isolation, so he began to go out more.

Every day he would talk to himself as he packed his lunch, walked to the park and had lunch on his favourite bench.

He had been sitting cogitating as he ate, when he became aware of her staring at him.

"Oh I am sorry," he said "have I been talking out loud again? I do that quite often you know. I suppose I was feeling sorry for myself."

George offered her a sandwich from his lunch box and was delighted when she took it from him.

As they sat quietly eating their lunch George learned that her name was Fay, so he introduced himself as 'Old George'.

Then he felt the need to explain why he was called 'old' George. He told her that he was seventy five or six years old but was not entirely sure of his true age.

Almost apologetically he explained, "When you get to my age you forget things."

Without giving away his thoughts, George felt that Fay had a 'bit of age' about her too. Maybe it was fashionable to be thin, but George was certain that Fay was too thin and a bit unkempt. But he kept those thoughts to himself as he offered her a biscuit from his box.

The day was pleasantly warm and they must have both dozed off. George woke with a start, surprised to find Fay still fast asleep. He shook her gently and told her it was time for him to go but perhaps he would see her tomorrow.

Next day standing in the kitchen, the talking out loud continued. "I'd better make a bit extra in case Fay turns up, God knows she needs a bit of fattening up." Then he began to worry, perhaps she was being neglected, or worse maybe she was sleeping rough.

The more old George pondered, the more worried he became. An old lady of Fay's age should not be living rough. He had no idea how old she was but she had the look of someone whose life had been hard.

By the time he reached the park he had woven a story of elaborate fantasy around his new companion, all without a shred of evidence.

Much to his delight Fay was standing beside 'his' favourite bench; she greeted him enthusiastically and old George grinned broadly.

Absentmindedly George began his talking, "I wonder what is in the lunchbox?" Fay was looking at him quizzically!

"I know, I know," he said, "I am talking rubbish again! Of course I know what is in the lunchbox, I made it." He went on to explain that he had lived alone and had done for six or seven years.

He began to tell Fay about his ex-wives and lady friends, but then thought better of it.

Silently he offered her a sandwich, helped himself to one and both new friends chewed contentedly. George offered some cheese and tomato but Fay showed little enthusiasm for them.

"OK my lovely, I'll have the cheese and tomato, you can have the roast meat sandwich."

Fay was most appreciative and again the old pair dozed off.

Over the course of the following two weeks old George learned most of Fay's foibles regarding food. She loved roast meat, chicken, lamb, cupcakes and custard creams.

Like many others she steadfastly refused to eat her greens.

Two weeks after their first meeting George decided to bring Fay home to meet the family; always providing she wanted to come.

Old George's son and two daughters were coming to stay with him for the weekend. George knew Junior would love Fay but the daughters might be a different proposition.

On Friday evening he explained his wishes and suggested he might bring Fay round on Saturday afternoon.

Junior was glad his father had found a companion but the daughters were more circumspect.

"What did he know about her? How had they met? What was she after?"

George batted all their queries into touch! Next day he explained his wish to Fay and she accompanied him joyously to his home, for the first time. To his great delight the girls approved, unreservedly, and Junior just loved her.

As he walked back to the park with Fay, George could barely contain his excitement as he told Fay of the impact she had made.

George left her at the park gates and returned to a happy, happy home. All three children were bowled over by Fay's friendliness and her cheery, outgoing personality. Then Junior laughed, "Why don't you bring her here to live with you; you would be great company for each other."

All night George lay awake considering the 'big question'. But what if Fay did not want to come?

George bade his children goodbye on Sunday morning and returned to talking to himself. "What if she did not want to come? Who would want to stay with a grumpy old man like him?" Then he reminded himself that he had not been grumpy since the day he met Fay.

He was filled with a strange reserve as he shared his lunch. Fay obviously, picked up on his mood, looking quizzically at him for several minutes, but George did not explain his mood.

As they ate George realised that he did not know where Fay lived. So having said goodbye he stepped behind some trees as Fay began to make her way home.

George followed silently, at a distance, until he saw her go round the side of a semi-detached house in a quiet street.

Giving her enough time to settle, George approached the house and rang the bell.

The door was opened by a very attractive blonde lady of indeterminate age. George guessed that she could be anywhere between forty and sixty years old. She had a friendly open face that radiated warmth and kindness, all projected in the simple, "Hello, how can I help you?"

"I'm looking for Fay," George began. "We meet in the park every day and I have grown very fond of her." The lady's smile broadened, "She is round the back," the lady explained. She used to live next door until her companion died, then she moved in here! The lady continued, "We had been very worried about her and she seemed to lose all interest following the death of her friend. We knew something had changed of late as she had started to put on weight and she became much more animated."

George looked rather sheepish. "It may be a shock to you but I would like her to come and live with me, always providing you and she agree."

George assured the lady that he lived nearby and she and her children could visit any time they liked. "Well," she responded, "we had better go and see what Fay has to say about it."

Fay was reclining comfortably in her chair, then she saw George; her delight was obvious.

"I've come to take you home, old girl," George whispered as he slipped on her leash

# The Baby Jag

I was not really eavesdropping on my wife's conversation as she whispered suspiciously into the phone.

She got like this every time a 'big event' was due and she had decided that this was the biggest of all.

I approached events with trepidation while she grew ever more animated. Her excitement was palpable while I felt only depression and a feeling of endings.

I had begged her, "Please no surprises, I want to forget that I am going to be seventy!" She had given that laugh that indicated that she either didn't hear me or simply ignored me. Over forty years I had grown good at being ignored so I raised my voice, quite considerably, "No surprises! Do you understand?" She nodded the blonde mop and schemed anyway. I must have entered the house more quietly than usual, only to find her doing what she does best, talking on the telephone!

She must have been engrossed as she evidently did not hear me but I heard her, "We are getting him a baby Jag." She glanced up, saw me and announced, "Have to go Anita." She searched my face for any sign that I had heard but I am well accustomed to hiding my feelings,

"That was Anita," she announced.

In my head I announced to myself, 'no it wasn't' but nodded vacantly. Calls to Anita always ended on an upward inflection and a cheery, 'see you soon!'

No, this was not Anita!

I was particularly vigilant, while feigning indifference to her actions. It was almost a week later when I next heard the 'Jag' word. To ensure maximum privacy she had shut the hall door (a rare event indeed) and carried the landline into the morning room (again closing the door behind her.) I waited a few moments before slipping out through the patio doors and strolling around until I was just beyond the glass side door of the morning room. At first the voice was indistinct but gradually I began to discern several words. For more than thirty minutes that scheming woman made six or seven phone calls, all containing the word 'Jag' and sometimes 'Baby Jag'.

Despite hearing the magic word on at least a dozen occasions, I could not stop the excitement that arose within me.

I had read about the new baby Jag which was about to hit the market. Strictly speaking it was Jaguar's new XE version, being brought out to compete with BMW's 3 series and Audi's A4's. It was the latest in technology, practically rust proof and surprisingly it was capable of more than sixty miles to the gallon. The dream machine was being provided in two litre, petrol and diesel engines but the acme was the new 3 litre model. Best of all, the entry price was 'only' £28,000 but I could dream about the three litre flying machine.

What a present! True my old X type was twelve years old and getting a bit tired looking but it had only sixty thousand miles on the clock. It had served me well and I would be sorry to see it go but how on earth could I refuse a brand new XE type? Then reality set in, how on earth could she afford such a gift? The answer of course, was that she could not. Hence the phone calls.

I slipped back into the house, via the rear door, and was casually sitting in my chair when she returned to the living room. I could not fail to notice the smug look on her face as I gloated inwardly. Of course, I would be suitably surprised on the day and I would be very grateful.

During the ensuing weeks I became increasingly guilty. My wife had just retired as a school teacher and my sons had very well paid jobs but my daughters were not rich. Even divided amongst seven of them each would be contributing more than four thousand pounds for the baby Jag.

I could not simply come out and tell her that I was in on the secret but I let my wife know that I would not accept any expensive presents. I'm not certain that I even convinced myself.

At one level I was appalled at the expenditure but at another I secretly coveted my new car; wondering about colour, cockpit and speed.

Then I began to wonder if they would give it to me on the day or must I be taken to the showroom to select my model? Now I was as excited as my wife!

The big day arrived and the clans gathered. The house is packed with children, grandchildren, brothers, sisters and I am suitably humble.

The children eat first, then the adults retire to the rarely used dining room for their treat.

Dinner finished, my wife taps her plate with her spoon to bring the assembled hordes to order. She makes a magnificent speech, peppered with anecdotes, humour, pathos and memories. She reaches under her chair and withdraws a large white envelope, "I know you said that you did not want anything special for your birthday but we would like you to have this."

She handed me the bulky envelope; my heart pounded as I accept her present, wondering if the keys were inside.

My fingers are trembling as I fumble with the envelope but eventually I manage to open it and extract the contents.

Staring up at me is a photograph of some tiny wild creature. My wife cannot contain her excitement: You have just adopted a baby jaguar. They are an endangered species in South America. The charity will send you updates on its progress and once a year you will receive photographs of your jaguar.

The assembled tribes are cheering and clapping. I fix a smile on my face and rightly claim, "I do not know how to thank you!!"

# The Birthday Boy

It all began several years ago. At first it sounded like an old style radio that was not quite tuned. A mixture of static, crackling and indistinct 'words' assailed me, coming out of nowhere.

The reason I remember the onset so clearly was due to the fact that I received the sounds on my twenty-sixth birthday.

At first I put it down to tinnitus and sought medical help for what I considered to be a middle ear infection.

Antibiotics, anti-allergic drops, home cures and prayer failed to remove the interference.

I sought specialist interventions fearing Menieres disease. Six months taking daily doses of serc made no difference whatsoever.

If anything, the interference seemed to be moving towards more accurate tuning. Amidst the whistles and crackling I could now discern distinct words. The words just popped into my head, with no relevance to what I had been thinking or saying.

Another visit to my General Practitioner elicited advice to play music softly in the background and the suggestion that I would stop listening to the sounds. I did not feel it opportune to inform the doctor that I had to cope with much more than sounds. At that stage I was still sane enough to know that any mention of voices in my head would result in a most unfortunate diagnosis.

Until my problem arose my life had been a joy, spending six months in Turkey, three months in the United Kingdom and three months in the West of Ireland every year.

A substantial legacy from my doting grandfather ensured I was never required to work, other than if I wanted.

And I did not want!

My father implored endlessly that I train as a carpenter in anticipation of my inheritance. Undoubtedly the furniture that he made was 'high end' stuff selling for small fortunes. But I had a large fortune, so I had inherited the earth. I suppose I could be described as an amateur geologist, ornithologist, archaeologist and several other 'ologists' as well.

Every day was joyful, free from stress, worries or the need to earn a living.

My father suggested that I should get married, settle down and start a family. Mother claimed that I had been put on earth for a much more important purpose. Despite pressure from my father, she was spectacularly unable to articulate what this purpose would be.

For myself, I was certain that I was much too selfish to share myself with anyone.

I had left the maternal home when I inherited Grandpa's mansion at the age of twenty-two.

The following year I purchased my belvedere in the North West of Ireland and finally a villa in Western Turkey when I was twenty-five.

It was with some pride that I maintained a staff full time in each residence and kept luxury cars in each country. If I thought about him at all, it was to bless Grandpa's munificence and his hard graft to accumulate many millions of pounds. I was even more grateful that he lived like a pauper in his mansion thereby ensuring my opulence.

Meanwhile the static and whistling became increasingly bothersome, interfering with my previously untroubled sleep.

An appointment at the private hospital resulted in the prescription of heavy sedatives. For several weeks I did sleep well; or rather for long periods.

Waking up was a 'drunken nightmare', despite the fact that I was teetotal. Another visit to the Consultant, antidotes provided for my drunkenness and I am back home taking two tablets every night. The side effects kicked in after two weeks with twitches, palpitations and an increasing feeling of depression.

Six weeks later I take myself off all medication and suffer the horrors of withdrawal. I eventually learned to start enjoying life again but the buzzing and ringing was back.

The only remedy, I felt was several months of sunshine. I flew to France, hired a yacht and crew and sailed around the 'Med', finally mooring near my Turkish villa.

The heat and light worked wonders on my tan and feel good factor but the buzzing continued. The Turkish doctor confessed to professional bewilderment as my description did not coincide with any tinnitus that he had treated.

Before I left his surgery he asked me to keep a record of the noises, especially any changes.

I have always believed that Turkey is best in the evening, the scorching heat of summer is replaced by a pleasing warmth accompanied by a refreshing breeze.

I was sitting on the patio, admiring the Aegean, the mountain and the long rows of olive fruit laden trees. The voice came out of nowhere, "This is where it all began."

Startled I looked and became aware of the 'Presence'; not a shadow, nor a breeze.

Just a presence

Then I realised that my buzzing was gone and I am on station. The words were spoken in my head!

I mulled over the words, "this is where it all began." What did it mean? What began here? Did life itself begin here?

I had no answers.

Several months and two plane journeys later I am sitting on a rock in Donegal when the voice returned, "Seek the light."

I look round but I am totally alone. I think this is becoming biblical but I know nothing about religion.

I enrol in a divinity degree, study the Torah. The Koran, the Bible in my spare time but do not find anything.

Well, not strictly true, aged thirty I am presented with a Bachelor's Degree in Divinity.

The words have been increasing of late, 'seek and ye shall find', 'I am the way', and 'come unto me' prevailed.

The harder I sought the less I found. Despair seized me as I searched around for the 'truth'! Dear reader, you have no idea how difficult it is to find the truth, when you don't even know 'What Truth'!

I decided there were too many truths to consider and I was much too lazy to enrol for a philosophy course. No doubt philosophy would have the answer but there was too much dross (for me) on the journey.

I much preferred the idea of a real, as opposed to a metaphorical, journey so I returned once more to Asia Minor.

I could not describe it as cogitating or meditating or logical analysis; others would see it as lying around doing nothing.

Whatever; nothing was what I did – a lot of it.

For no reason other than curiosity I decided to walk the 'path of Jesus'. I visited Bethlehem, Tel Aviv, Haifa and finally Jerusalem. I followed the pilgrim path to Gethsemane at the foot of the Mount of Olives in Jerusalem and remained unmoved spiritually. Back in Turkey I visited Ephesus, walking the same streets traversed by Saul of Tarsus.

I was at Troy when the voice spoke most distinctly, "Why do you look outwards?"

Having spent more than four years looking upwards, downwards, outwards and inwards I resolved to look no further.

I must have been dozing because I suddenly found myself suffused with light. A great sense of love enveloped me. The feeling of being encased within the womb embraced me as I returned to a state of innocence. The voice echoed from the heavens, "suffer the little children." I cried out in spiritual pain, "What do you want from me?"

The voice reverberated, "Carry my message."

I cried, "You have not given me a message."

I could feel the sadness of the Presence. Then I was left empty and alone as the Presence faded.

When I stood up I was purified; no, felt purified. I was pure, I was the light, I was love!

Was this my purpose in life? Must I preach love, purity and the search for light?

The answer was so simple that the question was not required. I would carry my message of love and light to anyone who would listen.

I wandered from village to village, town to town, totally rejecting my old lifestyle. I lived as the ancient prophets lived. I existed on nuts, berries, wild honey and the fruits from the sea.

Over time I was joined by a small band of followers, preaching peace, love, forgiveness and the quest for light.

My appearance changed dramatically. First it was the weight loss, then the growth of long, straggly hair and beard; then I abandoned my expensive suits and shoes and replaced them with simple robes and sandals. I lived in permanent ecstasy, sanctity oozing from every pore. Then I decided to visit the Holy City. My followers begged me not to, citing the many dangers that existed there.

I pointed out that I was sent to bring the message to everyone; Jews, Muslims, Christians and Atheists. My destiny had been decreed. For seven full days I addressed crowds who gathered outside churches, synagogues, mosques, market places and schools. Anywhere that people met I spoke. My message was simple; God or Allah or whomever sought peace and love.

The rioting started simply enough on my seventh night in the Holy City.

I was trying to give testimony of my search for the light when a young man, no more than sixteen or seventeen shouted, "Who are you to speak to us?"

I replied, "I have been chosen to carry the message." The young man yelled, "Charlatan, how dare you claim to be God."

I tried to tell him I was a mere man but the crowd had taken up a chant "Charlatan, kill the infidel."

The stones came think and fast. I implored my little band to leave and turned to face my accusers.

The blows were excruciating and unending. Everything went black.

When I awakened I am back in a private hospital in the United Kingdom. My mother and father sit by my bedside, each attempting to look more concerned than the other.

Dad opines, "Do not speak you have been sedated."

"What happened?" I manage.

"You were taken to a refuge in Jerusalem where you remained for three days until I came and spirited you away." I am still confused. "You have been raving for several weeks but you are safe now that you are home."

This did not feel like home, this felt like hospital. A tall distinguished gentleman entered the room, took my temperature and informed me that he would give me something to keep me calm.

I could see that something involved syringes, needles and drugs. I struggled to tell him that I did not need drugs, that I hated drugs.

His kindly smile left my mother in no doubt that these drugs were for my own good. I was so weak that I could not resist as he administered one drug after another. I began to drift into unconsciousness but I was certain that it was the doctor's voice when I heard, "I'm afraid there is no doubt your son is suffering from schizophrenia, he had delusions of persecution, visual and auditory hallucinations and a messianic complex." The doctor added, "He has disordered thinking, elevation of mood and very unusual behaviour."

My mother cries, "What is the outlook for him?"

The Medic adopts a 'caring face' and murmurs, "Not good, I'm afraid."

Then the other voice enters my head, "I did tell you to suffer the children."

"You did indeed, I think, as I slide into unconsciousness."

My mother's soft voice escapes me as she murmurs, "I wonder if he knows that this is his thirty-third birthday."

# The Camper Van

The advertisement was stark, 'For Sale. Volkswagen Camper Van; rarely used. Seven years old, two thousand miles, offers around £20,000'.

He gazed out of the window at his 'prized baby' and the memories flooded in.

He remembered vividly the day his dreams of travel began. He was eight years old when the horse drawn wagon rolled through his village. It was the first time he had heard the word 'gypsy'; he did not know that 'gypsy' was considered to be a derogatory term with Romany or Travelling People being the acceptable description of these strangers.

He ran alongside the leading wagon, marvelling at the bright colours and paintings on its sides; but most of all he was entranced by the piebald and skewbald ponies that drew the wagons.

He had stood, wide-eyed and open mouthed as the train came to a stop at the old dump. Each wagon disgorged what seemed like dozens of children and a couple of adults. The entourage had proceeded to relieve themselves by the side of the road, with a total lack of embarrassment. At the time he thought his mother would not have been pleased as not a single person washed their hands.

He watched awestruck, as horses were unhitched and led onto the grass, fires were lit and water boiled for tea. He was back next day to see the horses being re-shod; the heat of the smithy, the smell of the hot iron and pared hooves accosted his nostrils like nectar.

Everything was fantastic; the sounds, the smells, the strange way of talking and the almost naked children playing in the debris. All was magical.

On their second day he was allowed to come closer to see the men hammer out their tin mugs, baking tins, and tea drawers that they would sell to the villagers. He slunk behind the heavily clothed women as they went from door to door, begging for a few coppers. He had felt so sorry for the poor beggars who suffered insult and indignity from housewives who were almost as poor as the beggars themselves.

Then the wagons were rolling again. He knew not where but in that instant his dream was born. Someday, when he grew up, he would take to the road, going from place to place for the remainder of his life.

All night, in bed beside his sleeping brothers, he had visualised himself at the reins of his two piebald ponies as they answered his every command.

Just under ten years later he bumped into the most dazzling girl he had ever seen. As he turned the corner to access the shop doorway she tripped over the slight ridge above the top step and fell directly onto his arms. In the very few seconds that she remained there he had processed the wild red hair that fell in great rolls to her waist, the flashing emerald eyes and the long colourful dress that extended to her feet.

He had gallantly apologised for her misfortune as they both turned a deep shade of red. She mumbled something, extricated herself from his arms and turned to go. Despite only seeking to buy a packet of cigarettes, the shop was packed and ages passed before he was back on the roadside. He cursed his own tardiness, his stupidity for allowing her to escape. Then he glanced across the playground where she was flying on the swings. He watched in wonder as she sailed higher and higher. It was surely only a moment before she broke her neck. He rushed through the lynch gate and ran over to the swings crying, "Be careful Miss, that is very dangerous."

She laughed and called him a cissy.

Suitably chastened, he turned to walk away. In a flash she was beside him, announcing in a strange accent, "I'm Theresa, what's your name?" He noticed that she said it like There-ay-sa, not Ter-ees-a as the local girls did. He told her who he was and where he lived and then asked where she was staying.

He was bewildered when she replied, "Round past Paddy Mack's corner, as he knew that only two old men lived there. Before he had a chance to seek more information she challenged him to go on the swings to see who could sail the higher. He had been reticent, telling her that the swings were for children who were under fourteen years old and he was nearly eighteen.

"Well," Theresa announced, "I'm sixteen and a half and I am going on the swings!"

Desperately he announced that his family lived in a mill house and they would be evicted if he was caught breaking the rules. She laughed and said he was a loser but followed him as he left the playground. "Where are you going?" she demanded as he walked away.

"I'm going for a walk round the lake with you," he replied.

She had laughed out loud, a hearty uproarious laugh that made the hairs on his neck tingle.

"Ok," she said, slipping her hand in his, "let's go."

For one golden hour he had been in heaven, then she announced that she must go home. For the first time since they met her sparkle seemed to dim as she urged him to let her go on, on her own.

Though they had met less than two hours ago, he knew that he was in love. He could not bear to be parted from her and insisted on escorting her home. She had acquiesced but gained a promise that he would turn at Paddy Mack's cottage. He would promise anything for an extra minute of her time.

At the corner she pulled her hand free, stood on her toes and kissed him briefly on the lips before turning and running off around the corner.

He had stood with growing emptiness in his stomach and a desperate need to break his promise. He sprinted after her, calling "Theresa" at the top of his voice. She turned, a look of alarm on her face. "You must go," she whispered fiercely, "my father will beat me if he sees you with me."

He had drawn himself up to his six feet three inches and fourteen stone and announced, "No one will hurt you when I am around."

The he 'took in the scene before him'. Six fine wagons were drawn up in a line as ponies and horses grazed contentedly on the grass by the side of the road. A small rotund woman with rats' tails hair was climbing out of the rear of the final wagon. Her high pitched voice accosted his ears with a string of Anglo-Saxon expletives, although they sounded more like 'feck' rather than the usual inflection.

Theresa whispered fiercely, "Run before my father finds you." Just then a scruffy, dishevelled individual about fifty years old and five feet six inches came round the side of the wagon.

"Feck off, Gorgio," her father screamed. "You aren't welcome here. You," he roared to Theresa, "get in the wagon." Theresa stood still for a second and he whispered, "Will you come to the pictures with me tomorrow night?"

Her nod was almost imperceptible and her answer was only audible to him, "I'll see you at the bus stop over the hill."

Father was approaching and a small crowd of his companions were gathering but love can be stupid. Age seventeen years and eight months he stood his ground and bellowed, "If you lay a hand on her I will come round and kill you."

Father obviously thought that discretion was the better part of valour, as he turned and mounted the step into his wagon.

That night he had gone home on cloud nine; he had his first date. He also had his first disappointment.

At a quarter to seven next evening he had been standing at the bus stop in a state of nervous anticipation. Several minutes came and went and at half part seven he could contain himself no longer. He ran down the road, flying round Paddy Mack's corner but to his horror the wagon train had gone.

He had looked around him in desperation, taking in the detritus, the wagon tracks and the marks on the roadway where the entourage had taken off.

Frantically he ran to Paddy Mack's cottage demanding to know when the travellers had left.

"The damnest thing," Paddy Mack drawled, "They up and left in the middle of the night. I never saw the likes of it."

He had run all the way home, grabbed his bicycle and cycled to the nearest large town. Despite asking several residents, nobody had seen the wagons.

Each day for more than a week he rode North, South, East and West but it was no good. Theresa had disappeared, never to be seen again.

With the passage of time he gradually forgot Theresa but he never forgot the lifestyle she lived. He vowed that one day he would live on the open road.

Then life got in the way of living. Four years at University studying Economics was enough to kill boyhood dreams. Five further years being mauled by figures and finally he was a chartered accountant.

Parents, friends, uncles and aunts all congratulated him on his wonderful success as he was offered an appointment with one of the largest firms in the world.

For the next thirty years he crunches numbers, achieves promotion, becomes a junior partner in a life rich in mediocrity.

Through his twenties and early thirties he had joined the dating game but no one ever connected with him in the way that Theresa had. In his mid -thirties he decided that he was too old to hang about bars waiting to 'pull' recently divorced women; he poured all his energies into work, becoming a senior partner.

Aged fifty five he was working late, as usual, when he became aware of someone entering his office. Long ago he had decided that his office was a better place to be than the home that he had inherited from his parents. In the fifteen years that he had lived in his parents' home he had never painted, papered or changed a thing. Once in a while he rang an agency to send someone round to clean but it rarely looked any different from how he left it.

He ceased his musings to concentrate on the new entrant. "I'm sorry," she said "The supervisor said I should clean this office, I did not realise that someone was here."

"That's all right," he said, "just clean round me." Much to his annoyance, she chattered as she worked and he found it impossible to stop her.

She had only recently started this job, after her husband of twenty years had run off with someone else. She neglected to add that the poor demented husband had been heckled, humiliated, nagged and victimised by her caustic tongue for all of the twenty years.

She finished her diatribe by announcing that it was unlikely now that she would fulfil her dream of travel. Somewhere in the dark reaches of his mind the word 'travel' sparked a memory and he found himself describing his long forgotten wishes to travel.

Over several weeks he told her how he had invested in bonds and shares and had accumulated a substantial nest egg. He told her that in two years he would be retiring, drawing his occupational pension and spending the rest of his life travelling.

By now Marcia sat on the edge of the desk taking in every word. Setting aside their different stations in life, they had much in common, or so he told himself!

On the evening of his fifty sixth birthday he had no one with whom to celebrate so he asked Marcia to join him for a drink and dinner.

Marcia sparkled over dinner and responded positively to an invitation back to his house for coffee. She quietly felt satisfied by the appearance of the large Georgian house sitting in its own grounds. If the drab interior had an effect she wisely kept her mouth shut,

With suitable reluctance she allowed him to lead her to the bedroom. Twenty years of celibacy did nothing to enhance his performance but she expressed herself satisfied by her amazing lover.

Then they were an item; Marcia argued cogently that she could not continue in her present job while dating a partner. He could do little other than agree, settling a large allowance upon her.

With three months to go, prior to his retirement, they were quietly married in the local Registry Office. Four weeks honeymoon in a five star hotel in Antigua was spent in idyllic splendour before returning to the old Georgian house.

It was several days before irritation set in. Every day on return from work he would find an army of decorators, designers, gardeners and cleaners. He reasoned that the house did need a makeover but it was HIS house and he had a right to be consulted.

Following four weeks of frustrations and irritations he finally broached the subject of partnership with Marcia.

As he undressed later that night he had an old familiar feeling of disquiet; did she really mean it when she said as and from their wedding she owned fifty per cent of all he had! She had laughed but somehow it rang hollow.

Then the great day arrived; his last day at work, his first day of freedom.

Having made it through the presentations, the buffet, the glad saying, he exited from the building with two fat cheques in his breast pocket. One cheque represented his lump sum of three year's salary, the other thirty years of savings, bonds and investments.

At home that night he showed Marcia the cheque for three year's salary and she positively jumped for joy. At that time he was not sure why he kept the evidence of a much larger sum to himself.

Over dinner he told Marcia that he was flying to Bristol early next morning and their dreams of travel would become a reality when he returned. Her love making that night was the most passionate ever.

Marcia was still asleep when he slipped out of the house at seven am. He left the airport in Belfast and landed in Bristol at ten minutes past ten o'clock. The old dreams had returned in all their glory. For several weeks he had been liaising with the

Sales Manager about a brand new Volkswagen T2 camper van. The basic price had been twenty-five thousand pounds but the many extras added five thousand to the price. His 'baby' now had a space hopper for extra sleeping accommodation, captain's chairs which swivelled to form part of the cabin and a novel shower unit. He hoped Marcia would be as pleased as he was.

A short taxi ride and finally he was looking at his future. It was everything he had ever wanted, bringing back all the longing of youth and opening up all the dreams for the future.

Having waited for forty years for his dream, he decided that he should spend a little time on his own with the VW. He rang Marcia to tell her that he had been delayed and would need to spend a week in Bristol. She did not seem unduly concerned as she was tied up with hanging new curtains and installing new furniture.

He had groaned at her latest extravagance but at least he had one week to himself on the open road.

First he drove to Manchester and Salford to visit the home of his heroes at Old Trafford. Cross country to Lindisfarne and on to Berwick-on-Tweed followed by an overnight in Edinburgh and relaxation eventually settled over him. Then he crossed the country again into Fife, on to Perth then to the beauty of Fort William. He toyed with the idea of heading north to John O'Groats but finally decided that he must go home. All the way down to Cairnryan, across the sea in the ferry and home from the harbour in Belfast he tried to imagine the joy on Marcia's face when she saw the VW.

Just down the road from home he stopped in to the car wash to have the VW washed, polished and completely valeted. At last, pleased with the result, he slid silently up the driveway and parked right outside the front door.

Marcia was discussing new colour schemes for the new improved drawing room; she barely looked round until he told her that he had a surprise sitting outside.

Imagining a natty little sports car, she rushed outside, walking right past the VW.

"Where is it?" she demanded.

"Here," he said pointing at the VW. "All our dreams, sitting here on four wheels."

"What are you talking about?" she said.

"This is what we always talked about," he said, "you and me together travelling the world.

"That may be what you want. What I want is five star hotels, luxury cruises, first class air travel around the world."

He tried to bring a note of reason to her flight of fancy. "You saw my cheque and already you have spent almost half of it. Now we will have to live on my pension and enjoy trips around Europe in the VW.

"Enjoy!" she said, "ENJOY, you'll never catch me dead in that thing!"

He stood, staring blankly at her and there and then he decided to kill her. She had ruined his precious dream. He was a patient man, he had waited forty years to achieve his dream of travel. He would be patient but he would kill her.

That night and every other night he slept in the spare room. For several weeks he fretted over the 'modus operandi'. Then he got a job working in a butcher's shop. Over the ensuing three years he learned all there was to know about animal dissection and at sixty years old received his certificate becoming the oldest, newly qualified master butcher in the country.

His employer was devastated when he announced his resignation: not only was he popular with the customers and expert with the knife he also worked for half the salary of the other butchers.

He had been studying the small advertisements for several months before the ideal job presented itself. Tucked away in the corner it read, "Respectful, caring person wanted for night work in a pets' crematorium."

The owner was initially sceptical that a sixty year old successful accountant and master butcher would be suitable for the job of despatching cats and dogs to the animal heaven in the sky. The owner explained that there was little science involved; the dead animals would arrive at the crematorium to be boxed up and placed in the ovens. Afterwards the ashes would be collected in a box and returned for an appropriate fee to their owners.

The deal was swung when the sixty year old interviewee said he was writing a book involving crematoria and would work for free.

About the time he changed jobs he learned that Marcia was having an affair. Not only was she having an affair, they were travelling the world at his expense.

Still he bided his time until he was completely trusted at work. Increasing responsibility fell upon his shoulders until he was the sole despatcher of overnight cases. At home he sat and planned. First he bought a chest freezer as he would only be able to dispose of her body little by little. For some time now he had been reading books on human anatomy and comparing humans with the carcases from cows, sheep and pigs and goats.

He was fairly certain that he could bring in lunch box size chunks of her, cremate that part along with a dog or cat and separate the appropriate amount of ashes afterwards. No one was going to do DNA checks on ashes to see if it really was their cat that was cremated. To test his theory he brought in half a chicken in his lunch box, cremated it along with a cat and guessed the amount of ash that he must bring home. It all went like clockwork.

Soon it would be time to put his plan into action. With his butchery skills, his deep freeze and his knowledge of cremation it should be straight forward.

Then his whole plan was ruined. Two sombre looking policemen rang his doorbell just as he was sharpening his knives.

As soon as he saw the solemn look on their faces he knew the game was up. But how had they learned of his intentions? He had told no one.

The senior policeman asked his name and having been told, said "I'm afraid your wife has been killed in Italy."

The shock was palpable, his delight almost impossible to hide. The policeman added, "I'm sorry Sir, it appears that she had a lover who knifed her to death in a violent row."

"Oh my God," he gasped. "Can I bring her home?"

His heart sang as the policeman suggested cremation in Italy, with the ashes being flown home the next day.

When the funeral director delivered the ashes he managed to maintain an appropriate expression of sadness.

For several weeks he laboured in the VW. Neighbours were sure it was only to assuage his grief. Several new pipes and heaters were added to the VW together with two fire blocks which could be inserted in the newly installed wood burner.

At last he expressed himself satisfied. He smiled to himself at the thought 'that nobody would catch her dead in that thing'. But there she was, scattered all around it.

The VW sold the following day of the advertisement. He watched her disappearing into the distance and smiled at the thought that she would hate it. He smiled some more.

A few days later the huge Winnebago was delivered, bought with some of the life insurance money resulting from her death.

He could not stop that smile, regardless of what the neighbours thought.

Tomorrow he would be on the road. A 'Theresa' was out there somewhere; he was a patient man.

# The Dream

## 1840

The voice is urgent and compelling, "Save the children, save the children." For three nights in a row I have been having the same dream. I wake in a sweat at the horror of the images that I have just witnessed. Potatoes rotting in the fields, cattle are dead or appropriated to pay rents, coracles/curraghs have been removed by the agents and people starve in the midst of plenty.

The sea is alive with mackerel, pollack, lobster, crabs, and salmon but without the little boats they cannot be fished. People are dying from starvation and disease; the graveyards are full and bodies lie dead by the side of the road, in houses and fields. A million people are dead and another million are fleeing to Scotland, England and America.

Ireland is awash with misery, yet still the absentee English landlords demand their pound of flesh.

I struggle to my feet and cross to the kitchen table where I swallow a pint of cold water. I gaze around our little cottage, to the children sleeping on stilted frames around the upper parts of the walls. My wife, Marianne and I sleep in a curtained off section in the kitchen/living room. Our home consists of this one room, lighted by a single candle and one tiny window to give light during the day. A bucket, placed in the sheltered area outside, is our toilet on those occasions that we do not relieve ourselves at the side of the fields.

Over half the parish is owned by Lord Hill and I am one of his tenants, farming four acres in a system of Roundel. I have one acre of land high up in the bog, providing turf to heat and cook all year round. I have a further two acres of good arable land where I can raise cattle that pay the twice yearly rent to his Lordship. My final acre is by the sea, around the cottage; the land is rich and fertile providing prodigious quantities of potatoes that comprise our staple diet. We eat potatoes three times daily, consuming upwards of thirty pounds each, every day.

On good calm days I take the coracle out to fish, often landing as many as a dozen Pollack or mackerel in one day. Fish that are not eaten are salted and stored for later use. I grow some corn on a piece of reclaimed land that I have been given permission to drain and use. Marianne is a fine hand at the milking; she makes bread, cakes and porridge from the fruit of this reclaimed land.

I look at my four fine sons, plump and healthy snoring contentedly in their childhood dreams. Then there is little Seaneen, not fit, not healthy who shares his parents' bed. He has a terrible cough and needs medicine but we have no money for such niceties. The doctor has told us that Seaneen will not survive the winter and the priest advises us to thank God that we have four other healthy sons. I know that I will be damned to Hell for my wicked thoughts but in anger, I silently scream, "Why cannot a merciful God give me five healthy sons?"

The priest had visited several times over the previous month offering platitudes like, "Mere men cannot know God's holy will" or "The child will soon be in a better place." Inwardly, I damn God and scream that my son cannot be in a better place, than with his father.

Marianne comforts me daily, she points out that Lord Hill is a good and kind landlord and that our sons will soon be able to join me in the fields, but I want a better life for them.

I step outside, immediately cooling in the fresh Atlantic breeze. The moon is on the descent and daylight will soon bring another day. The water laps gently, rippling over endless numbers of rounded rocks. In a few months the sea will be a raging torrent with one hundred miles an hour winds battering the coast. But, the crops will be saved by then and the cows safely tucked away in the byre that abuts the house.

I am lost in thought as I gaze distantly, imagining that I can see America's shore, five thousand miles away. Legend has it that America is the land of plenty and already four of my brothers live there.

My mind slips back to the days when all nine of us lived with our parents in this little cottage. Times had been hard then, with recent religious conflicts still alive in people's minds. Previous friendships where neighbour helped neighbour were replaced by suspicion and hatred. Protestants now kept to themselves and Catholics sought to build their own schools and places of worship.

As a boy I had witnessed lean years, where the blight damaged the harvest but nothing like the devastation that I had experienced in my dreams.

When I had told Marianne of my first dream she had laughed, "Should we build an ark, like Noah and sail away?"

As the dream recurred I began to see sense in Marianne's assertion; not to build an ark, like Noah but definitely to sail away.

I was so engrossed in my thoughts that I jumped when a hand touched my shoulder. "Another bad dream?" Marianne asked.

I waited for a moment before speaking, "It would take little to change to leave us vulnerable."

"You are such a pessimist," Marianne responded. "We have enough turf drying to last for two years, we have four fine cows, each with healthy calves to pay the rent and potatoes enough to feed the parish."

I felt foolish as I explained, once more, that my dreams were prophetic. In the olden days the same dream, three nights in a row was regarded as proof of a coming event. I also pointed out that I had noticed an increase in the rainy days over the past three months. The rain had been relentless, just as it had been when I was a boy and September had brought the dreaded blight. I told her how we had almost starved that winter. Without the help of our neighbours most of our family would have died. Nowadays folk were less likely to help one and other. Then I blurted out, "I believe an angel is telling us to leave."

Marianne blessed herself and gasped, "Sean Og, how can you say such a thing?"

I put my arms around her in the hope of giving her some comfort. "I know bad things will happen if we stay."

Marianne looked up through tear strewn eyes, "Then let God's holy will be done." She blessed herself again and returned to the warmth of her bed.

I stood silently, beneath the stars, wondering if it was God's holy will or mine.

Rising early I walked to the house of the agent for Lord Hill. I told him of my plans and sought to clarify the extent of my debt. When it was all settled I was left with three cows, a calf, twenty four lines of turf, an acre of healthy potatoes and several hundred weight of grain.

Next I visited the local headmaster to seek his advice about where I should go. The teacher had been active in the risings of 1798 and 1803 so England was out of the question. Scotland was England's lackey, so America it must be. He pointed out the many difficulties, not least getting to a deep water port. Donegal had no such ports, nor had she the boats to sail to large ports. Neither path would be easy, we could walk to Sligo, down the west coast or cross country to Derry. If we chose Derry, we must first sail to England before embarking on the outward journey.

As I mulled over my dilemma the Master added that I must beware of thieves, vagabonds and jackanapes all along the way. He emphasised the need to keep my money well hidden, never letting anyone see notes and always bartering when trying to make deals.

The picture painted by the school master was so bleak and drear and filled with terrors that I was almost on the point of abandoning my dream. Then he added, "If I was a young man like you, I would risk all to provide my children with a better way of life."

A note of nostalgia entered his voice as he described his early life 'on the run'. He had been only sixteen during the '98 rebellion and almost twenty two in the '03 rising. Following that failure he had fled to New York, then south to Maryland, then Virginia and then eventually all the way to Texas.

He had worked on construction sites, in factories and cattle ranches before training to be a teacher. He emphasised his regret at returning home after twenty glorious years but he had married an Irish immigrant with a yearning for home.

I finally got a 'word in'. "So you would definitely go?"

"Without a shadow of a doubt," he answered.

I had one further question, "Sligo or Derry?"

I got a schoolmaster's answer, "Its fifty odd miles to Derry and more than ninety to Sligo. You cross mountains to Derry and the road to Sligo is a nightmare. You sail directly from Sligo to New York but Derry only takes you to Scotland or Liverpool in England. So Derry takes two sailings but the choice must be yours."

My head was throbbing by the time he had finished.

Then I made the mistake of asking him how he had got from Ireland to New York.

His reply was the fierce rebel once more, "Under a tarpaulin in a fishing smack to France, by foot, horse and canal to Spain and on to America."

The route did not appeal.

Marianne and I discussed our proposed route long into the night. Finally she rose, stretched her arms above her head and announced, "I'm off to bed Sean Og, and you decide and tell me in the morning."

Typical woman, I thought always opting out of the big decisions. But, then it was my idea after all, so it was right that I should choose the route.

The days passed in a flurry of activity, first to go were my fine fat cows, at a poor price. None of my friends had money and I could not travel on credit.

Just under one month later we set off on foot for Derry, stopping first to say a prayer at our parents' graves. The weather smiled on us as we traversed the single track route past Errigle and Muckish. At Termon we untied our packages and had a hearty meal of bread, warm milk and salted mackerel. We made the children as comfortable as possible on beds of heather and ferns and settled to spend the night under the stars.

On awakening Seaneen's cough had worsened and he burned with fever. All morning he was delirious but no relief existed in that wild countryside. We found a doctor in Letterkenny but by then it was too late. Seaneen died aged ten months in that doctor's front room.

The parish priest muttered a few prayers over Seaneen and sought assurances that we could pay for a Mass and a grave in consecrated ground.

All day and night we knelt by that tiny grave saying our goodbyes and reassuring Seaneen that we would meet again. It was Paeder, our eldest son who spurred us into action. "If we are going to make Derry before nightfall it's time we were on our way."

A silent sad troop started the final leg of their journey in Ireland. Marianne was the first to sag, after fewer than five miles. Drawing me to one side she announced, "I am with child again." I did not know whether to laugh or cry, having just buried one baby.

I drew her to me and cried, "Everything will be alright, just wait and see." To my great shame I committed my first crime that very day; seeing an old pram outside a farmhouse, I crept over and stole it. With a little ingenuity I was able to break off the bottom end, cushion the top and provide Marianne with her very own man-powered chariot. With the younger children taking turns in our chariot we made good speed arriving at a tavern on the outskirts of Derry while it was still light.

We all agreed that a good night's sleep in proper beds would do us the world of good. The inn keeper was a shifty eyed, rough looking character but he assured us of comfortable beds for the night. We agreed to his charges but first sought restorative food.

We were engrossed in our tasty stew when a young man, of probably twenty one or two joined us; apologising for the interruption. He introduced himself as Sean Gallagher from Cresslough and declared that he had heard the inn keeper and four rough looking cronies planned to rob us when we had gone to sleep.

Now the headmaster had warned me of this ploy, where a seemingly innocent person alerts you to danger and helps you to escape. The innocent stranger then knocks you on the head and leaves you for dead.

To my great shame this is exactly what I thought when I first met Sean Gallagher. I decided to play along slipping most of my money, unseen, to Marianne. At an appropriate moment I told her to divide the money among the boys' clothes, without anyone becoming aware of her intent. Having finished our meal. We paid the innkeeper, gathered up our belongings and headed for bed. As soon as the innkeeper left, we slipped down the stairs and out the back door, where Sean Gallagher was waiting.

All night I watched him with great suspicion and on the morn my suspicions grew when he suggested a different plan of action. No boats were sailing for Liverpool that week, so Gallagher suggested we make our way to Belfast, where regular sailings took place. I looked at Marianne for guidance but she was no help at all. With his clear blue eyes, open countenance and wild red hair Sean Gallagher did not look like a footpath; but then, how did footpaths look?

Belfast was more than seventy miles away, much of it over rough tracks but Marianne assured me, with the help of the rusty pram that she could make it.

The walk was uneventful save for the second night, spent in driving rain at the top of the Glenshane Pass.

Sean Gallagher worked like a Trojan pulling bushes together, lying ferns for beds and covering all with great sods to provide a water tight shelter. How could I have suspected that good man of criminal intent? In truth he was our guide, mentor and leader all the way to Belfast and on to Liverpool.

It was Sean who found the way to Waterloo Docks in Liverpool, accompanied us on to the Philadelphia, a fine sailing vessel who would take us and two hundred and twenty others all the way to New York.

Steerage was cramped, unhygienic and overcrowded where the poorest passengers slept, ate and socialised in the small space. On entering the ship each steerage passenger was given one week's supply of provisions; five pounds of oatmeal, two and a half pounds of biscuits, one pound of flour, two pounds of rice, half a pound of sugar, half a pound of molasses and two ounces of tea. With seven of us travelling together I felt we were well provided for. Problems arose when we cooked; there was only one tiny cooking room about twelve feet by ten. Naturally everyone wanted to eat at the same time which was impossible. Over the course of two or three days this problem worked itself out, mainly to everyone's satisfaction.

The passage to America was anything but joyous, with seasickness, illness, vomit and smells of urine filling the air with stench. The ship was at the mercy of the winds and the journey took more than four weeks, by which time more than half the passengers in steerage had gone down with sickness. Twelve days out of Liverpool, Marianne started to bleed and, due to lack of privacy, next day everyone knew she had lost her baby. During the worst of the storms we were confined below decks, sometimes for days on end. Time allocated to go on deck brought instant cheer, this allowing the worst excesses to be removed from our living/sleeping areas.

With much relief we sighted New York, nearly seven weeks after leaving our Donegal home.

It is no exaggeration to say that Sean Gallagher was our life saver. Without knowledge of the great city and having no one to greet us, Sean took everything in hand. His cousin Ruardi met us at the wharf, welcomed us like his own family and lodged us with a second generation Irish/American lady in Manhattan. Marianne and I could hardly believe our good luck. We had a sitting room to ourselves, two bedrooms, a small kitchen and a bathroom that was shared with three other families.

One week later Ruardi had fixed Sean and me up with jobs on a construction site and the boys were attending school for the first time.

At twelve and ten Paeder and Seamus were most indignant to be placed in the same class as their six year old brother Hugh. Three year old Con helped Marianne fill her days in her new and overwhelming city.

Time sped and suddenly a year had passed. Now all four boys were at school; Paeder and Seamus had leapt ahead. Paeder was particularly keen on learning, spending every spare minute in the library. Seamus, always the practical one made toy guns, sabres and showed an aptitude for carving. Hugh and Con enjoyed their childhood.

I had saved quite a bit and felt sure that in two or three years we could have a place of our own. Sean Gallagher visited every week, much to the boys' delight. No visit passed without some gift or plaything as the children took to calling him Uncle Sean; a sobriquet he did not try to deny.

The first sign that something was not right was when Marianne developed a cough. Then she got night sweats and the cough became productive. The sputum fell like silver sixpences, finely flecked with blood. The doctor was blunt, the TB was far advanced. Marianne would have to go into a Sanatorium. The treatment was not cheap and there was no guarantee of a cure. There was no question, our savings would be provided and Uncle Sean chipped in whenever he could. The cool fresh air of the Sanatorium, together with good food and caring staff saw Marianne improve and her doctors were hopeful of a cure. However Marianne must stay in the retreat for nine to twelve months to effect a cure. Every weekend Sean, myself and the boys journeyed to see Marianne. Every weekend seemed to show some improvement, then six months into the treatment I got a telegram stressing the urgency of a need to visit. Marianne had had a massive haemorrhage and had not recovered consciousness.

I gathered my clan around me and we sped to the Sanatorium. As we entered the room, Marianne sat bolt upright and gasped, "Take care of my boys." She fell back into her pillows, never speaking another word. Marianne died at four the following morning, if she had lived for two more days, she would have been thirty five.

We brought Marianne back to New York and had her buried in a plot that I had bought that very day. The last words that Marianne spoke was a plea to me to look after her boys. To my very great disgrace that is exactly what I did not do.

When the funeral was over and the mourners gone, Sean, Ruardi and I headed to one of the many Irish bars around Manhattan. At thirty five years of age I got my first touch of alcohol. The fiery whiskey burned into my soul, driving away the demons that gathered there. Much to my undying shame I neglected my family and lost myself in an alcohol haze. I remained in that haze for six months, finally begging on the streets for the next drink.

I was lying semi-conscious in a pool of my own vomit when I became aware of a large pair of black boots at eye level. "Get up you dirty drunken Irish scumbag. You're a disgrace to your country, your family and yourself." There was no escaping the harangue. "I've had my eye on you for some time and you are no damn good." I struggled to a sitting position but the bile overcame me and I covered his shiny black boots. "Now look what you have done you dirty scoundrel. Clean them up," he shouted throwing me a rag. I struggled to complete the task but fell back exhausted.

"Right scumbag," he drawled, placing his truncheon under my chin, "get up or I swear I will kill you with this pig-stick."

I struggled to my feet, balancing on wobbly legs. "Ok, scumbag it is the nick for you!"

"You can't do that," I cried, "I have four children at home who are dependent on me."

"Then God help them scumbag with a waster for a father like you." Then he demanded, "Who is looking after them?" I had to confess that I did not know.

"No, I suppose you don't, scumbag, and what do you care anyway."

I fell over the edge, the sobs fell in great gulps as I lost all self- control. I was vaguely aware of falling down and crawling into a ball. It all came out, "My dead baby in Letterkenny, the miscarriage on the ship and the unbearable loss of my darling Marianne."

His voice took on a softer note, "Right Sir, stand up we are off to the station. What is your name and where do you come from!" he questioned. I gave him Marianne's pet name for me.

"I'm Sean Og from Donegal who are you?"

"I'm Sergeant Mick O'Shaughnessy from Dalymount," he said in that peculiarly lyrical Dublin accent. He added, "If you have any complaint to make, you can do it when we get to the station."

"I have no complaints," I answered.

At the station he led me to a cell and left me alone without locking me in. He returned at seven am with steaming hot coffee and toast. I accepted the coffee gratefully but declined the toast with a shake of the head. The coffee helped, so I struggled to my feet. Another mug was offered and accepted and my world stopped spinning.

"Right," he said, "stand up and raise your arm?"

Before he finished I gasped, "Am I being arrested?"

"No," he said, "you are being enlisted into New York's finest and if you let me down I will personally batter you to death. Now say after me ---." So I did and became one of New York's beat cops.

The look on my children's faces when I made it home on shaky legs told its own story. Again I burst into tears. I begged for forgiveness and swore I would never touch another drink. I was amazed at the smart appearance of the apartment and the cupboards filled with food. It took little detective work to realise that Sean Gallagher had stepped into the role of father when I fell through my own particular hole into hell.

It took time but trust was rebuilt. Sean claimed he knew that I would come through but did not think it would take so long.

There is little else to say about me. I collected my uniform on the Monday following being sworn in. I tramped the beat for five years before making Sergeant. For twenty five years I modelled myself on Sergeant O'Shaughnessy, without the 'scumbags' and I believe I did a good job.

I lived through turbulent times as a policeman. At fifty two I was too old to enrol when Civil War broke. In many ways I was glad I did not have to fight as I was not too sure where 'right' lay. My beloved second son, Seamus, gained entry into West Point and had been a serving officer for nine years at the onset of hostilities. I am blessed by the fact that he survived the carnage, retiring as a full Colonel in 1865. Sad to report my dear friend Sean Gallagher was Seamus's Sergeant, falling at the Battle of Potomac, posthumously receiving the Ribbon of Honour for bravery above and beyond the call of duty.

My eldest son, Paeder, whose first schooling happened at twelve years old continued his studies eventually becoming Professor of English at one of the elite universities. Blessed with two fine sons and a beautiful daughter he lives a short bus ride from me.

Much to my chagrin and due entirely to their mother's influence both Hugh and Con entered the Priesthood. Hugh is Dean of the Cathedral and Con has spent his life in the Mission fields.

I bought this house, with its front porch and rocking chair for Marianne. She had been gone for ten years before I could afford it. Nowadays as the moon is rising, I talk to her, reminding her of the sun setting over Inishmore and the moon rising over our little cottage. I ask her if she remembers the bog, growing corn, making bread and I sense her smiling.

In 1843 the light of my life left me.

In 1880 the light went out.


2012

I'm thirty-two years old and acting the fool with my friend Chris. Chris is twenty years older than me but younger in so many ways. He is irrepressible, optimistic, outgoing and the best friend that any man could have. We spent the best part of ten years traversing the globe, then we went our separate ways. Chris headed to Hawaii and God knows where else.

At present he has houses in New York, Los Angeles, Paris and Turkey and is rich beyond our boyhood dreams. He is married with a baby son and for the first time ever seems to be settled and happy. Unlike Chris I have not made an impact anywhere. I'm single, never having contemplated marriage, foot loose and usually broke. Others would probably describe my ways as feckless but I have never experienced anything that lit up my life. That is not to say that I have not enjoyed myself, I have and I have wonderful friends. It is just that I have never felt fulfilled.

As usual Chris is playing about with his electronic wizardry as I chide him for his inattention. Chris's booming laugh fills the room. "It's only Facebook man, my Bro is sending some photos." A sunset shot fills the screen and the words tumble from my lips, "That is Iniserer." An image of a little cottage comes up. I gasp, "That is our house but someone has raised the roof." Chris is looking at me in the strangest way and then he asks, "How can this be your house Seanie, when you have never been to Ireland." A not unreasonable question I had to admit but that is my house. Chris asks if I want to speak to Bro but it is unnecessary. I know where I am going and I know how to get there.

I 'tap' Chris for five grand and fly to Dublin. I take the bus to Letterkenny where I hire a car. I drive North West for the best part of an hour, arriving at Teach Jack's just before sunset.

I drive down the laneway, turn right at the lake and on past the school. I stop at the V junction and gaze out towards the ocean.

The light comes on.

# The Fateful Day

The days of our years are three score years and ten;
and if by reason of strength they be fourscore years,
yet is their years labour and sorrow; for it is soon cut
off, and we fly away.

Psalm 90 v 10
King James Bible

My life has been one of fortunate coincidences, lucky
breaks and sometimes monumental setbacks.

I have lived that life by my own rules, neither seeking
nor giving favour. I have never suffered fools lightly but
strove to live by a code of honour. While honour has
been my driving principle I have not always lived up to
the standards that I have set myself.

I have caused immense hurt and bitter disappointment
but never deliberately set out to hurt anyone. I have
never felt the need to prop up my life with mythical
symbols, organised religion or spiritual claptrap.

I have always sought to be my own man, relying totally on my
own resources.

How strange then that I should be moved by words
that were first written thousands of years ago.

We had been clearing out my father-in-law's last home
and my wife had relocated much to our own home.

I picked up a dusty old King James Bible that fell open
at Psalm 90. The words of verse 10 leapt out at me:-
"The days of our years are three score and ten; and if
By reason of strength they be fourscore years, yet is
      their years labour and sorrow; for it is soon cut off, and we
fly away.

      For the first time in my life, words spoke directly to me.
      I am nearing the fateful three score years and ten and my
years are already filled with labour and sorrow.

      I re-read "labour and sorrow" and find a solution in "for it
is soon cut off and we fly away"

      I ask myself if the words give permission for one to cut off
one's self from the pain? Or perhaps the clergy are correct in
claiming that only God can choose the time and method of our
parting.
      But what makes them experts, and what is the situation if
one does not accept the existence of God?
      I reflect on the labour and sorrow! I list my ailments;
arthritis, asthma, insomnia, postsurgical nerve damage, angina,
alimentary polyps and unending pain in my back, legs and
shoulders. Bedtime is a nightmare of restless legs,
sleeplessness and endless tiredness. Then there is the anxieties,
the constant and often losing fight against depression, the
hopeless, helpless feelings of loneliness that is pathological
and the intrusive suicidal thoughts.

      Again I consider the words "labour and sorrow; for it is
soon cut off."
      I dwell on the ethical question of whether or not I have the
right to end this sorrow?
      Who or what gives me the right?

Who or what denies me the right? Do I control my own destiny or is my fate predestined by some remote and apparently uncaring God?

There are no absolute answers! Some distant primeval teaching alerts me to the wrongness of even considering such a question. Yet haven't I always been a pragmatist; haven't I always lived by the use of practical means and expedients.

Then I remind myself that, while I like to consider myself to be practical there have been many times when I have allowed my heart to rule my head.

But what if heart and head are in total agreement, what then?


Even if I was a Christian, how can ending the suffering be considered sinful?

"It is soon cut off and we fly away" If this is the written word of God, it does not prevent me from 'cutting off' what is not wanted and is no longer useful.

If I was a Christian I might argue that 'cutting off' this hateful thing would bring great relief and a better life for my wife and children. I might even argue that it is a God-like thing that I do!


But I am not a Christian; I am not anything, other than an empty shell in a sea of turbulent trouble.

I must make my decision. I must face the fateful day alone and unaided. The easy part of the decision involves the 'how and when'.

My cowardice precludes blood, hanging, shooting, drowning or jumping from a great height. This leads to drugs.

I have access to vials of morphine, left here following my mother's death. I have two full cartons of morphine prescribed when I left hospital following a botched knee replacement operation. I have ten full boxes of co-codamol and assorted other medications.


I have the how at my disposal. The when will arise when my wife flies to England to visit our daughter and grandchild.

Locked doors will convince casual callers that the house is empty. The when has been chosen.

I grow tired of my planning and faux- philosophising and retire to the kitchen. As I sip my tea another coincidence presents itself. Lying on the table is a National newspaper where the front page proclaims that researchers have developed a single jab to fight arthritis. Hope springs momentarily, but inside tucked away on page four is the reality the jab will be available in two to five years.

I briefly consider that this God, mythical or otherwise is teasing me. Teasing is a much too gentle word, taunting more readily fits the bill.

I'm back in my considering mode. Several passages from the Old Testament present a fearsome God: a God of retribution, not to be trifled with.

The New Testament presents a God of love, a kindly old gentleman who reminds me of my grandfather. This God is benign and loving.

I wonder why he changed? Then I realise that it is man who has changed. After all HE is constant, unchanging, omnipotent, omniscient. No, HE did not change.

Then my thoughts drift to cause me to consider why we call God HE?

No, HE reads much more like a SHE; subtle, patient, abstruse, controlling, clever, always considering the 'angle'. Yes much more SHE than HE.

I shake myself out of my reverie. Why am I arguing about the gender of a Myth? If such an entity existed I imagine that it would be neither HE nor SHE.

But I can't help wondering if this spirit would be retributive or loving!

Like St Paul, I cast off the things of childhood and apply analytical thinking to my dilemma.

The irritations of everyday life interrupt my reflections. I fulfil my husbandly role as best I can, including driving my wife to the airport.

I am back at my desk and, for the hundredth time I pick up the consultant's report. It starts innocuously enough, so I scroll down to the important bit -----

My cancer is stage 4, it has spread from my bones to my bowel, lungs and brain – there are no treatments available.

I read the last line again, 'there are no treatments available'!

I reflect on the fact that I would be three score years and ten in three months' time. Surely God would not be pedantic, after all what is three months among friends.

I try the old Bible again. It opens at John 8 v 32:

"And you shall know the truth and the truth will set you free"

The way ahead is clear!

# The Ghost

## Prologue

The horror of life in the 'Poor Houses' of England and Ireland is well known. Through media of film and television most are all too aware of the indignities suffered by the 'Magdalenes' in the convents and orphanages throughout Ireland. Less well known is the 'care' provided for children who were unfortunate enough to be diagnosed as lacking in intelligence.

Regardless of cause, these children were categorised as cretins, morons and 'feeble' minded with their fate being a life in mental institutions, where they would never exit the building, except in death.

Mental institutions continued to be grim places throughout the 20th century until the advent of major tranquilisers in the late 1950's. By the mid 1960's mental hospitals were 'open' places where patients could move about more freely.

Not so for the newly categorised mentally handicapped/special care 1, 2, 3 who would never feel grass under their feet, nor splash in the sea, nor enjoy visits home. No, these were the forgotten people. Many blind, deaf, anencephalic, microcephalic, epileptic ----- and all alone in the world.

Parents were often advised not to visit and siblings were often unaware of the existence of a handicapped brother or sister. Specialist hospitals and units were developed, but many hundreds of mentally handicapped patients continued to be contained in 'back wards' in mental hospitals until as recently as thirty years ago. The 'Grange' in this story did exist and did contain the people that I describe. For several reasons changes have been made to names and locations.

It is hardly necessary to say that the 'ghost' is a figment of my imagination. Almost everything else is true.


# The Grange

The only grand thing about the Grange was its name.

It was about 60ft long and about 15ft wide with toilets and washrooms 'tacked on' at either end. It was situated well to the rear and apart from the rather grand red brick Georgian building that was the local mental hospital.

By the early 1970's the mental hospital prided itself on being a leader in its field. No one mentioned the Grange that was somewhat different.

And it was different in so far as that it housed 'severely mentally retarded' patients rather than those who were mentally ill.

The building comprised 3 sections. To the left were contained 'burned out' schizophrenics (many of whom had had major leucotomies), several 'simple souls' and a residue of people with general paralysis of the insane (a condition resulting from untreated syphilis). Many were known by nicknames including the 'Buck Goat', 'Horse' and 'Hippo'.

The central section was the nurses' office, staff toilet and clinical room.

The section to the right had eight severely retarded 'boys'. The overall ambience was the pervasive acidic smell caused by years of urine that had filtered into everything. The only ventilation from the toilets was through dormitory windows.

James first entered the Grange as a young staff nurse in 1970. It was a Sunday morning and the air was rich with odours of urine, faeces, vomitus, perspiration and overall decay.

Despite having trained for three years and worked for some more years in Geriatric wards, James' first reaction in the Grange was to seek out the toilet, where he was violently ill.

The elderly senior staff nurse was reassuring, informing him that he had little to do, except help with feeding the patients. James could not believe what he was hearing "little to do, all the 'wee boys' were doubly incontinent and two had vomited over the bedclothes.

The older man explained, "Old Jimmy will clean up the boys." Old Jimmy was a long term patient, who was diagnosed as General Paralysis of the Insane. And clean them he did.

Jimmy had a plastic pail, some soapy water and one very dilapidated cloth. Methodically he worked his way through the eight boys, washing them each in turn. No attempt was made to prevent cross infection, with Jimmy using the same cloth throughout and only changing the water when it turned dark brown in colour.

Old Jimmy changed the boys into clean nightshirts, provided by the nurse, while James and his senior colleagues converted the bed settees back into settees, upon which the boys spent their days. Despite being saturated with urine, no attempt was made to 'sanitise' the bed settees.

Then the Senior Nurse left to attend church, leaving James alone with his new charges. James was standing in the middle of the chaos of stinking bed sheets, soiled clothing, faecal covered floors and the air rich in the ammoniac smells of urine when a domestic assistant entered the building and asked if he wished to have some tea and toast.

James sensitive stomach surrendered; he rushed once more to the bathroom where he was violently sick for the second time in two hours.

When he emerged from his exertions James found the domestic lady standing at the office door laden with teapot, cups, milk, toast and jam. James mutely turned and re-entered the bathroom.

This time the domestic was gone when James made his re-entry into his new world. Obligingly she had left breakfast cooling in his office.

Old Jimmy fed his 'boys' with porridge, bread and tea all contained in large bowls. Some of the mixture made it into the mouths of the boys but much was sprayed round their faces, new night shirts and the general surroundings. James was watching this debacle when the senior partner returned from church. "Don't worry" he offered, "they will eat it up over the course of the morning."

James lurched back to the bathroom but had no further stomach contents to discharge.

At lunchtime a mixture of soup, potatoes and mince was mixed in large bowls and again old Jimmy did the feeding. Prior to distribution the Senior Nurse had added large quantities of tranquilising drugs to the dinner mixture.

James was horrified but the older man was reassuring, "This was the only way the boys would take their drugs."

James had protested that it was illegal to 'hide' drugs in food but his older colleague just laughed and informed him that he 'would learn'.

Over the following three weeks the older nurse spent most of his time in his office reading his Bible. Every suggestion for improvement, made by James, was met with absolute rejection.

Then fate kindly intervened; the senior nurse took ill and retired on grounds of chronic sickness. James was joined by Tom who was only four or five year's senior to him.

Tom's induction followed similar lines to James' earlier troubles.

For two days the young men recorded the routine undertaken by old Jimmy, listed changes that they wanted to make and developed plans to meet their objectives.

Initial requests for supplies to Senior Managers were ignored or rejected so new strategies were decided upon.

Top of the priority list was the removal of the stinking bed settees and replacement with proper beds.

James returned from the pharmacy in a state of high excitement; he had detoured via the stores on his way back and discovered a plentiful supply of hospital beds and mattresses.

The mental hospital had replaced all hospitals beds with modern divans and the old hospital beds were just 'lying' around.

All day Tom and James laboured carrying 20 beds and mattresses to the Grange; then they dragged out the old bed settees and deposited them behind the Grange.

The beds, mattresses and waterproof covers were duly installed but seating was now required.

Over the course of a week Tom and James 'stole' chairs from the great hall, from other wards and from the back stores. In two weeks each resident had his own bed, chair, locker and washing materials.

Then the two nurses decided that they must destroy the settees else senior management would put them back in situ.

James favoured spontaneous combustion in the hot sun as both knew their jobs were on 'the line'.

Spontaneous combustion was aided by a gallon of petrol from the boot of James' little Morris Minor.

The smoke was black, acrid and could be seen for miles. The senior manager rushed to the scene, summoned the Fire Brigade and sought an explanation.

Whether he believed in spontaneous combustion James and Tom never knew but he did not step inside the Grange to see conditions for himself.

Next on the list was proper clothing, cutlery, plates, cups, saucers and a varied menu. With some ingenuity all were acquired together with tables at which to dine.

Despite all efforts the Grange still stank. With all foul smells escaping from toilets at each end of the building; the consequences were inevitable.

Once more fate took a hand. The hospital inspectors made an unannounced visit. Accompanied by Matron, the dignitaries were shown round; one inspector looked directly at James and asked," If you had your way here what would you do with this place?"

James had not yet learned the politics of obfuscation. Frankly he answered, "If this was a building that housed animals it would be condemned. It is not fit for human beings and should be razed to the ground." The shocked look on Matron's face told James he was in trouble!

The inspector added, "In the meantime what would you do?" James replied bitterly, "Put two windows in each bathroom, install proper showers, have dividers between each bed, put vents in the ward to allow stale air to escape, place two more staff on each shift and start proper continence programmes."

The inspector smiled, "That is quite a list, and we'll see what we can do."

Over the ensuing weeks the windows were fitted, the vents installed and two showers placed in each bathroom. Then the improvements stopped.

James took it upon himself to seek out the Principal Tutor with a view to having student nurses 'placed' in the Grange. James argued that therein was truly intensive care nursing and the Principal agreed to think about it.

Then the Matron sent for James. He was sure that he was in trouble.

For the first time ever James was invited to sit down in Matron's huge office. James' heart raced. Matron began, "You have done a great job but now your skills are needed elsewhere. I am sending you on a management course to prepare you for promotion. When you return you will take charge of ward x."

While pleased, James had a sinking feeling of betrayal, "What will happen to the Grange?" he said.

Matron announced that the Grange would be 'razed' to the ground and a new purpose built facility would be erected.

James went on his course and was promoted. Then he went on some more courses and got more promotions. Aged forty nine James was near the 'top of the ladder', then massive reorganisation was mooted.

James was tired, wanting no part in the latest change; he sought early retirement.

The Chief Executive granted James' request but informed him he had to work until his fiftieth birthday. James thanked his superior and requested leave to work as a staff nurse in the facility that had replaced the Grange. This request was considered to be decidedly odd but no objections were raised.

James spent an enjoyable ten months back with his 'wee boys'. Despite his previously elevated status James slipped easily into his role as team leader for the six remaining severely handicapped patients.

Despite the severity of their disabilities James was convinced that they could hear and respond to him. He read books to them, played music, sang little ditties and used touch as a means of communication. Pascal, the youngest of the six, responded to 'Old McDonald's' farm by waving his arms and throwing his legs in the air. James was the only one who saw Pascal smile.

The months rolled by with James providing a role as parent, carer, cook, cleaner and companion but soon it was time for him to leave.

For two weeks prior to his retirement James told his boys that he would be off on holiday for two weeks but assured them nightly that he would be back each night to get them ready for bed.

Night staff were only too happy to have James work in a voluntary capacity.

Sure enough two weeks after his retirement James returned. Staff did not pay too much attention to his comings and goings, as he quietly went about his work.

Each night just before 8pm James would appear, prepare supper for his fold; making sure Les had his cocoa, John his Ovaltine, Pascal had his hot milk and the others had their tea.

Then he would help them to bed, sit in the middle of the ward and tell them little bed time stories. Occasionally he would sing and always he would wait until all were fast asleep before he slipped away quietly.

Every night for ten years James continued to provide his unique brand of care. With the passage of time the boys' numbers had been reduced by deaths and now only Pascal remained.

The ward sister felt that it would be appropriate to mark James' unique contribution with a little party to mark his sixtieth birthday and his ten years of voluntary service.

To maintain utmost secrecy she told no one of her plans, other than in the vaguest of terms.

She wrote to James' wife inviting her to the ward party without any indication of its purpose. Sister's plan fell nicely into place when she received Jane's (James' wife) positive response.

All day she laboured, preparing food for the feast, then to her horror Pascal quietly expired just before Jane's expected arrival.

As usual James arrived just before 8pm to be told of Pascal's death. He begged Sister's indulgence asking if he could have a few minutes alone with Pascal.

Sister left him with his grief and returned to the office where she could see him stroking Pascal's hand.

Then the doorbell rang and Jane was escorted into Sister's office.

"I'm terribly sorry," Sister explained, "We have just had a patient die so a party may not be appropriate."

Then the soft baritone voice could be heard, "Old McDonald had a farm eh, hi, eh, hi, oh and on this farm he had some ducks….."

"Who is that?" asked Jane.

"That is Pascal, the gentleman who has just died," Sister replied.

"No who is the elderly gentleman who is with Pascal?" asked Jane.

Sister looked strangely at Jane; perhaps her eyesight was failing her.

"That is James," said Sister.

"James who?" asked Jane.

"Your husband James," replied Sister as the baritone voice continued to assail them.

"That is impossible," replied Jane. "James was involved in a terrible car crash on his way to London, two days after he retired. He spent six months in a hospital for brain injured patients before coming to a Nursing Home near to our town. James has had 'locked in' syndrome for ten years without ever being able to communicate with anyone."

The strains from 'Old McDonald' faded away and Jane knew that when she turned round James would be gone. Tonight he would be with all of his boys.

# The Kindly Killer

The Publisher's text is succinct: 'Your leading character lacks charm.'

To say that I am bemused is the greatest understatement of the year.

I fire off a text, 'explain please?'

I wait in vain for the rest of the day.

I text back, 'What is it you want?'

This time the text is more direct. 'We cannot publish the manuscript in its present form.' He stresses the need for romance, warmth, kindness otherwise the readers won't buy.

I am even more gobsmacked. I text, 'Are you sure the previous text was meant for me?'

I receive a one word answer, 'Yes!'

I spend several hours re-reading every word of all seven hundred pages. I have set out to create the vilest creature in the history of crime thriller fiction.

I have created a back story of a child abandoned by a feckless father, abused by a sadistic, alcoholic mother. He's been abused physically, psychologically and spiritually by a series of his mother's 'friends'.

Isolated at school, he is the bad boy that every parent has warned their child about. The only emotions he knows are anger, aggression and the adrenaline rush that comes with violence. As one, he is the school bully and the school 'cowardy cat'.

By the age of twelve he is hooked on violence; breaking the bones of his school mates is no longer enough. He seeks new ways to find his thrills.

He finds a bag of abandoned kittens that somehow avoided the drowning for which they had been intended. A gorier end awaits them.

The first kitten is placed in the washing machine, the settings moved to the highest temperature and the machine switched on. He watches fascinated at the kitten's desperate and futile scrambling. Having satisfied himself about this form of killing he places kitten number two into the freezer. He finds this less satisfying as he cannot witness the kitten's suffering. He boils a large pot of water, drops number three into the pot, slamming on the lid. He watches enthralled through the glass lid at the terror within. He is particularly pleased to see large clumps of hair fall off the poor animal.

He has reserved his most horrific experiment for kitten number four. He cleans out and resets the wood burner with fire lighters, coal and wood. To this nest he adds the final kitten and lights the firelighter.

With enormous detachment he sits back and watches the kitten's curiosity turn to fear and then abject terror. He smiles beatifically throughout his experiment.

There is no guilt, no remorse. No feelings of shame. Just an overwhelming feeling of power. He is in control, he holds the power of life and death over these creatures.

He resolves to bring the same power over people when he is older, bigger and stronger.

Meantime he refines his 'art' by killing birds, poisoning dogs and cats and bullying all the weaker kids he crosses.

At fifteen, I had him fully grown, street wise, clever, vicious and ready to start on his new career.

The first time is an opportunistic 'kill'. His mother is off working, probably on her back, while her friend is inside stoned 'out of his head'.

The main character creeps into the bedroom and soon finds needles, syringes and the 'makings'. The boyfriend doesn't even move when the needle is plunged into a vein, the heroin works quickly, so 'our hero' leaves the syringe and needle in the arm. Turning up his nose at the smell of sweat, stale drink and God knows what else, he finds himself a half full whiskey bottle. He dispenses the spirit round the victim's body and over the sheet. He lights a cigarette, places it in the ashtray, dribbles a little lighter fuel on the burning ember and waits.

He remains in the room until the bedclothes are well ignited, exits the back door and scarpers. Several hours later he is back home, witnessing the devastation. The street is cordoned off but a policeman is able to tell him that a drunk had set himself on fire and burned to death.

To his great delight he learned later that the boyfriend could only be identified by his dental records. He mentally marks off ONE in his memory box.

Mother and he are re-housed and he decides that it is time for her to go. Another fire is out of the question so he follows her on her way to work. Keeping well behind her he follows her into the underground. He is standing right behind her as the train thunders through; the slightest of nudges and she is under the train wheels. Number TWO he thinks and rejoices that he has the house to himself to pursue his career.

Four black college girls are murdered and the police are seeking a racist suspect. In the interest of fairness the next four are white working class females.

The police are seeking a misogynist loner as none of the girls had been sexually assaulted.

The next four have traces of seminal fluid, some inserted before death, some afterwards. He doesn't care what tests the police conduct as the seminal fluid does not belong to him.

The police produce a very accurate profile. A young man, abandoned as a child, a loner, emotionally cold and a history of violence.

He adopts a new persona. He dates girls. He is utterly charming, always moving at their pace, never sleeping with them until they wish it. He is a gentle, caring lover, generous with his time and money until it is time to dispense with them.

No, he never harms them that is not his modus operandi, he only kills strangers.

He ends his relationships with poignancy; he is being transferred overseas, his firm is moving to New York, Calais or Perth. Numerous girls kiss goodbye to the love of their life.

Meanwhile his career 'flourishes' over more than five hundred pages. He shoots, stabs, poisons, garrottes all with equal efficiency. He has catholic tastes when choosing his victims, black, brown, yellow, white, Christian, Muslim, Sikh or unbeliever, he slays them all.

He is driven by one ambition; he wants to make Geoffrey Dalmer and Dr Shipman look like amateurs.

He is fully cognisant of the fact that by choosing strangers, the likelihood of being caught is slim.

He knows that others have killed more victims through bombing and mass killing but he wants the record for singles and doubles.

In the interests of equality he murders children, adults and the elderly with equal aplomb. Heterosexuals, homosexuals, a-sexuals are all on his hit list.

Seven hundred pages of unadulterated evil and now the publisher wants the main character humanised. Impossible!!

Then the ending presents itself.

The main character is back at the shallow grave that he has just dug. His latest victim has just died the death of a thousand cuts. She looks almost serene in the moonlight as he gently takes her hand. He thanks her kindly, begins to cover her with stones and ferns and says, "Have a good day now!" before smiling and walking off into the moonlight!!

# The Perfect Crime

How does one commit the perfect crime? And what if the perfect crime is murder?

Detective thriller writers, police and scientists are adamant that the perfect crime is impossible.

Shooting, stabbing, drowning and poisoning are out; but what is in?

Surely my First Class Degree should provide the brain power to achieve my objective but the harder I think the more pessimistic I become. Anyway what would Psychology provide that would outwit the combined forces of law and order, pathologists, toxicologists and various forensic scientists?

I ponder the problem for several days but every scenario eventually hits a brick wall. It just cannot be done without getting caught!

Nevertheless I cannot escape from the thoughts that have become obsessions.

There has to be a way!

What has caused me to reach such a state of potential lawlessness? Nothing other than my 'beloved' daughter-in-law.

Right from the start I was never sure of her suitability for my kind gentle son. She arrived too soon following the break-up of a five year love affair; love on the rebound I suppose.

With undue haste she rushed him up the aisle in a flurry of expensive gloating. No doubt in my mind, she had caught her man: son of rich parents, highly professional with excellent prospects. No, he was not going to escape.

Six years and four children later, she turned off the tap; separate beds and he could like it or lump it. She had long since given up work to indulge her expensive tastes, huge home, expensive furnishings, luxury cars, nothing escaped her avaricious eye. Maids employed, gardeners, handymen without ever giving a thought to my son's ability to meet his outgoings.

Too proud to ask for help, my son works ever longer hours, while his 'beloved' wife does less and less. It begins with a whinge that she is exhausted caring for the children, so my son agrees to make dinner when he gets home. Then he gets to bathe the children, get them ready for bed and tell them bedtime stories.

All this he does uncomplainingly.

His chores continue even after the youngest child starts school. If he wonders what his wife does all day he keeps it to himself. Long ago he learned that anything is better than his 'beloved's' moods.

For ten years I have remained in the background silently fuming. Endlessly I ask myself why he will not 'stand up' to her. But I know the answer; he loves his children too much to risk losing them. I try, ever so subtly to tell him that his children are being damaged by their cold and unloving mother, but he argues that they have a loving father.

And he is right, but not right enough!

So why now, after ten years in the background am I scheming to bring about her death?

The answer is easy really. My beloved grandson got sick on holiday. Rather than offering love or showing sympathy she moaned about the cost of the holiday.

It took all my resolve to keep from slapping her but a dark sinister idea was born.

I WOULD KILL HER!

For weeks I pondered. A hit man seemed like the best idea. But where do you get one? Do you look him up in Yellow

Pages under murder? Even if I found one how could I employ him (or her) without ever meeting or giving away a clue to my identity?

I devoured murder mysteries, spent hours watching old murder films on TV. Despite the seeming perfection of some of the plots, I saw problems with all of them.

Perhaps the experts were right, perhaps there was no such thing as the perfect crime! I eventually concluded that the only way to escape justice was down to luck.

So I stopped obsessing. I was happily dozing in my favourite armchair, in that strange place between sleep and awake when the answer crashed in.

So simple, so pure, so undetectable that I leapt out of my chair with a great "Whoop," startled the dog who scampered behind the settee.

The more I thought the more perfect it sounded. It would take time, it would take guile and it would take great patience.

I would get her to murder herself!

I think to myself, 'slowly, slowly catch the monkey'. First I acquire an old but perfectly serviceable mobile phone, with no links to me. I absolutely refuse to tell how I came about it; perhaps not entirely legally. I spend days teaching myself how to send text messages. At last I am ready; the text is short but not so sweet. "You know everybody hates you!" I smile to myself as I press send.

I wait

Several days later I receive a phone call from my son. He is incredibly tactful. He tells me all about his wife's 'hate mail' and concludes by asking if I know anything about it? I feign indignation. How would I know anything about it, I do not have a mobile phone and I have no idea about texting.

He apologies, lamely, claiming it might have been my idea of a joke.

Again, I feign indignation, claiming that I may have a strange sense of humour, but I am not, sick.

He apologies profusely.

I arrange to call and see him and the family. The mobile phone has been dispensed with, now resting at the bottom of a very deep lake.

I ring and arrange my visit.

I am laden with goodies for the children, cake for the tea and flowers for my daughter-in-law.

I play with the children, chat with my son, and then settle restfully into a deep armchair.

I fix the daughter-in-law with my thousand yard stare. I can feel her become aware of the stare as she shifts restlessly in her chair. She turns and gets the full focus of 'the stare'. I lower my eyelids slightly, tighten my mouth (just a little) and maintain the stare. The colour drains from her face and I know that she knows the origin of the text.

I increase the fierceness of my stare. She gasps, "Is there something wrong?"

I reply that I was concerned by the lack of colour in her cheeks.

My son agrees that his poor wife does not look well.

I excuse myself, telling them I must go and let the poor dear get some rest.

I smile inwardly as I drive home, knowing what the topic of conservation will be in my son's house.

The phone is ringing as I enter the hallway and I have no need to check the number.

My son launches in, "My wife says you were staring at her."

Truthfully I reply that I was. Less truthfully I add that I was concerned by her poor colour. Then I begin to sow the seeds; "Is the poor girl well?" I ask," first I am supposed to have sent some sort of text message, now I am staring, one assumes in a bad way." I continue, "Could it be some sort of post-natal depression or some sort of grief reaction because all the children are at school?"

I fill my voice with concern. "I cannot think of any reason why the poor girl should have these paranoid ideas about me."

I plough onward, "Is it only me or does she feel this way about others? I did notice that she was sharp with the children and she did seem to be critical of you!" Then I round it off, "You must not worry, I'm sure it's only tiredness, she will be back to normal in a few days."

There it was, I had laid down the marker, the poor dear is not normal.

I wait a few days, then ring and invite them for dinner. I know the children love to visit their Grandpa as they can play with dogs, cats, horses, paddle in the river and frolic in the indoor pool.

I hear cries of, "Yes please" in the background and wait for the visit. As expected my son visits but pleads sickness on behalf of his wife.

When the children are dispatched to their various activities I ask, "Is she still paranoid?"

I notice with some satisfaction, that he responds, "Yes" without hesitation.

I pretend sincerely and ask if it is getting worse?

"I think so," my son responds, "she picked a fight with one of the school teachers and sacked the maid. " I ask why?

I can barely contain my glee when I am told that the maid 'took my son's part' when 'darling wife' belittled him. I ask about the teacher and even I am shocked by the answer. "She thinks the teacher hates her because we are well off and a higher status than she is."

I think it is time for another phone call!

I know she has a 'lie down' every day after lunch. I wait until I think she is settled and ring from my house phone. Following several rings the phone switches to answer mode but I am not that easily put off.

Following four attempts the phone is answered with a shrill "Hello."

I am sympathy personified. I beg forgiveness if I disturbed her and continue to talk. I speak slowly and calmly, not providing her with an opportunity to blame me for anything. I enquire after her health. I ask about the children continuing to speak in a calm and warm voice, I finish by wishing her a speedy recovery from whatever is bothering her.

My son rings me later in the evening asking how I felt about his wife's health.

I hesitated just long enough to allow doubt to implant itself. I say, "Sorry son but I kept a recording of our conversation, just in case the paranoia presented itself."

My son offers no protest as I finish by saying that I think she is much better.

I'm back on the phone again, having disturbed another midday sleep. It takes a little while but eventually she calms down. I go through the usual routine, offering the same platitudes. I speak slowly in a low voice to ensure she does not get upset.

I speak for some time with only the occasional 'yes' and 'no' coming back at me.

I know from her responses that she is in a more positive frame of mind and much more relaxed than she was yesterday.

I continue calmly and warmly ensuring that she registers everything I say. Eventually I tell her that I must go and she should forget all about phone calls as they upset her so much.

I am interrupted by the sound of the house phone. My son is in a terrible state, he describes how his beloved wife went for a walk after dinner. Some beachcomber found her body at the bottom of the cliff. My son doesn't know if she jumped or fell but she was dead on impact.

I offer him and the children my condolences and a promise for whatever support was needed. "Of course they are all heartbroken," I agree then that time is a great healer.

The policemen, pathologists, toxicologists can test for evermore if they wish. As yet no one has ever been able to design a test that would detect post hypnotic suggestion.

# The Robin

Tommy 'Tucker' Taylor was the scruffiest boy in the school. In fact most people agreed he was the scruffiest child in the South of England.

Tommy earned his nickname four years ago during his first year at school. The teacher spent most of her time announcing, "Tommy Taylor, tuck your shirt in, Tommy Taylor tuck in your shoelaces?" The list was endless and that is how he became Tucker.

It was not that Tucker was neglected: quite the reverse in fact. Each morning his mother saw him off to school immaculately dressed. No, it was just that circumstances always seemed to contrive to mess him up.

Tucker's world was the world of hedgcrows, copses, furze, trees and riverbanks. He loved them all and was drawn irresistibly to them. Tucker was fascinated by the 'life' that existed in this other world and just had to follow sounds into the furze. He had to climb trees in the off chance of seeing nestlings or run along the riverbank to watch the trout rise.

No matter how early he left for school he was always distracted and last to arrive. Assembly was a nightmare as he would amble in, with strange green foliage in his hair his jacket dishevelled and his shirt hanging out. The assembled throng immediately sang out, "Tommy Taylor, tuck your shirt in!"

This morning was no different. He had heard a fluttering in the hedgerow and just had to investigate. Having fought his way through foliage and thorns he spotted a badly injured bird. The little creature's breathing was much too fast, there was blood around his head and one wing was badly damaged. On closer inspection Tucker could see that the little bird was a Robin and several of his feathers were lost.

The little creature was too weak to resist when Tucker extracted it, stroked its poor injured head and placed it gently in his pocket. He supposed the tiny bird had been mauled by a cat.

Tucker did not hear the usual cry as he ambled into assembly. He had more important things to think about. He knew that he must not let the teacher know the secret as the robin would be taken from him. Tucker decided that his father was the only one he could trust. He nodded sagely to himself, 'Dad would know what to do'.

Tucker behaved furtively all day, avoiding his classmates and friends. At break time he waited until everyone had left the cloakroom before slipping in and washing the blood off the robin. Tucker tried to give the bird some water but it was unable to drink. The day dragged by interminably, with Tucker watching the hands of the school clock, as though hypnotised.

At last it was time to go and Tucker left 'on wings'. Without speaking to anyone he ran all the way home, praying that Dad was home from work. His luck was in.

The words tumbled from Tucker's lips in great volcanic explosions. Dad signalled, "Slow down, speak slowly!"

Eventually the whole story tumbled out, the robin was extracted from the pocket and Dad commenced his examination. "Poor little thing," Dad whispered as he gently took the bird from Tucker. Dad eventually spoke the dreaded words, "I do not think your robin can be saved but let's see the vet."

The vet's examination confirmed Dad's suspicions; the little bird was too badly injured to survive. The misery in Tucker's face spoke volumes. The vet also had a nine year old son and he would be heartbroken at the loss of such a beautiful creature. The vet continued his examination, all the while absorbed in Tucker's misery.

"All right," he said, "let's try something."

Firstly he allowed some gaseous thing to calm the robin down, then taking a pipette, he dropped a little fluid into the bird's mouth. Finally he made an improvised plaster cast from cardboard and thread and announced that that was all he could do. He warned Tucker that the bird might well be dead before morning but if it lived, it would need to be fed with worms, flies and seeds.

Tucker was more than willing to be caterer for his new friend.

Over the ensuing days Tucker was later them usual for school but did not share his secret with anyone. Each morning he dug for fresh worms, dropped water into the invalid's mouth and gently stroked its feathers. Dad had turned an old shoe box into a nest, lined with cotton wool it was the perfect indoor resting place. But the natural habitat of robins was outside, not indoors. Dad discussed the problem with several other residents who dutifully trooped through the house to visit the invalid.

Two weeks into rehabilitation the robin stood and took its first tentative steps and Dad and his friends got to work.

Paper and pencil was produced and a grand three roomed nest was designed. The carpenter from three doors down turned the design into a wooden reality. A heavy plinth supported a stout wooden post, topped with living quarters. The living quarters consisted of wood on three sides with glass to the rear. The wooden roof was detachable and the front door was a hole that was small enough to prevent access by predators. The rear room was sleeping quarters, lined with leaves, straw and twigs; the middle room was bare to allow walkabouts. To the front was a platform from which the robin could view the world.

The new home was situated in Tucker's garden, well hidden by leaves, ferns and bushes. Neighbours drew up a rota for feeding 'their' bird that could not yet fly.

The weeks passed and robin grew stronger and braver, walking to the very edge of his platform. The seasons changed and now it was winter.

A soft flurry of snow encased the garden in a world of white. A heavy night frost froze the flakes to crystal, then robin took his first flight.

First he flew to the wise old owl, then to his long missing friends. In the language of all flying creatures he explained his absence and told everyone about his luxurious living quarters. Friends listened enthralled by the kindness of the human creatures, especially Tucker. All agreed something must be done.

In a flurry of activity the little robin and his friends collected great quantities of deep red holly berries and set to work. All night they laboured to complete their task, then with the first pale rays of sunlight they sang their chorus.

Tucker woke with a feeling of excitement as he always did on Christmas morning. He leapt out of bed, drew his curtains and stared in wonderment. There in the garden in less than perfect symmetry the bright red berries spelled out their message –

Merry Christmas Everyone.

# The Speech (For Gary)

This is simply the hardest thing I've ever had to do. Perspiration flows from my head in torrents, my mouth is dry and my stomach in knots.

My blue shirt is obviously unsuitable for the drama ahead. Ten seconds after trying it on and it is saturated. If I am like this in my own bedroom, what will I be like tomorrow in front of that scary audience?

I roar for my wife. She does what she always does, she ignores me!

I yell again in desperation.

1. She pokes her head round the room door and demands, "What?"
2. "What will I wear?" I cry in total despair.
3. Not unreasonably the 'Better Half' asks, "Do you want formal, smart casual or just casual?"

"How am I supposed to know?" I ask.

Again she is very reasonable, "If you don't know, how am I expected to know?"

"Always the same," I mutter, "NO help at all."

"Ah well, if that's how you are going to be I'm off," she responds.

Talk about cutting off your nose to spite your face, now I am in real difficulties.

I adopt a wheedling, pleading tone, "Please help me darling . . ." but she is gone.

I'm a grown man; I can do this – suit, smart casual, casual. Jeans and moccasins would be too informal, so that just left suits or jacket and trousers.

I'm sure I have had more difficult decisions to make but I cannot think when.

I can feel myself becoming bad tempered. I drag ten suits from the wardrobe, raging at my wife's profligacy. She is forever buying new clothes for me. I immediately reject three suits for being too shiny and one for being 'bally'. I resolve to get rid of them but absentmindedly return them to their place in the wardrobe. I measure myself against the remaining six suits, eventually whittling my selection down to a blue pinstripe and a very fetching Magee tweed.

I'm on the point of berating my wife again for her profligacy, then remember that I bought the Magee on a trip to Donegal.

I call her again. "The pinstripe or the Magee?" I ask.

My wife looks with obvious discernment. "I think a jacket and trousers might be better. Under the circumstances I think a suit might be too formal."

Under what circumstances I think and follow up with, "Why must women be so frustrating?"

I throw down the suits on the bed and cry, "Which jacket?" She runs her hand along the rail; three Magee's, two Charles Tyrwhitt from Jermyn Street, a Savile Row number and several less expensive brands. She extracts an elderly corduroy jacket claiming, "This might do."

My blood pressure goes through the roof. I start to speak or rather splutter. She laughs and withdraws the special Savile Row jacket and says, "This will be perfect."

To circumvent the next question, she hangs a pair of slacks against them and pronounces them to be a perfect match.

Thankless creature that I am, I demand "What shoes, black or brown?" She provides the shoes – navy!

"Should I wear a tie?" I squeak.

She withdraws two ties from the rack and suggests I put them in my jacket pocket, only deciding on the day.

A normal man, or a man in normal circumstances would relax and spend the evening with his wife enjoying television.

But this is not a normal man and these are not normal circumstances, so I have another shower, redress and examine the notes I have made for the big occasion.

I read through my fifteen pages of notes and add a few more. I dash into the living room and ask my wife to listen.

I can tell from her expression that she had 'turned off' by the time I was on page two. Panic is instantaneous and accompanied by a throbbing headache.

If I cannot maintain my wife's interest what hope have I with tomorrow's more discerning audience?

She is a teacher, for heaven's sake, so I ask her advice.

"Bullet points might be better," she suggests.

Bullet points, bullet points, could she not have told me yesterday?

But then, I did not ask for her advice yesterday.

I get back to work. It is approaching midnight when I approach her with my revised 'cog cards'.

She is less than pleased. "I was almost asleep," she muttered. "What do you think?" I plead.

"Too many cards," she claims, "and you need to build in some questions."

"Please help me?" I beg.

She reluctantly crawls out of bed, skims over the 'cog cards', discards most of them and scribbles a few ideas.

"How long is your speech?" she asks.

"About forty five minutes," I answer.

"Will you take questions throughout?" she adds.

"Yes of course," I reply like an expert.

She discards more cards.

I finish with two cards, five bullet points and five questions.

"You will probably only get through three or four" she sighs as she crawls back into bed. I mutter thanks.

I put my original eighteen pages, thirty 'cog cards' and her two final versions into my briefcase.

I have another shower, towel myself and don a dressing gown.

I check I have the right date, the right venue and the right time.

I am re-reading my notes when my wife reappears.

"Are you coming to bed?" she demands.

"In a moment," I reply, "just some last minute checks."

The 'Better Half' draws herself to her five feet five inches.

"Is this the man who addressed a thousand delegates at a recent National Convention?"

I nod.

"And was it you who was chief speaker at the Professional Forum in London, and did you have work published at home, in Spain, Mexico and the United States?"

I wonder where this line of thinking is going. I agree that I have had some experience of public speaking and writing.

I stare at her, amazed at her lack of understanding. Yes I had spoken to groups in excess of one thousand but did she not understand this was an invitation to the most difficult audience one could imagine?

Tomorrow I have to address my son and his classmates!

# The White Lady

I have often thought of daybreak as the rebirth of the world. I watch in wonder at its birth, development, decline and death in the endless cycle of life. Birth is best, with first feeble rays streaking across the sky. I have watched in wonder at that thing called daybreak and been moved close to tears by God's wondrous hand.

In the three years since my ordination I have risen each morning, in darkness, to ensure that I would be in position to witness the daily miracle of the world's rebirth.

My old friends in the city would laugh if they could see me now, labouring daily as a curate in this little country parish. Much hilarity had arisen when the 'head boy' at the seminary failed to achieve a plum posting. It mattered little to me where I was employed doing God's work.

The posting was not without its difficulties. The Parish Priest was elderly, traditional and resentful about the placement of a young 'happy clappy' priest. For forty years he had managed perfectly well on his own and, if he was a little forgetful, his flock were happy to accept his eccentricities. Despite his protests, the Bishop insisted in installing me as curate, with the good canon very firmly in charge.

My first day had been filled with an exposition of the canon's rules. There would be no 'happy clappy' music, the choir and organ were the only instruments of God's voice. The clerical collar would be worn at all times, no fancy sports shirts and trainers in this parish. Sermons would last for exactly thirty minutes and would focus on God's punishment for wrongs. There was no place in this church for a milk sop God of love and understanding. There would be no hand shaking in church, nor jumping up and down like Protestants. I disagreed with everything he said and almost everything he did but I had to learn humility. At least that is what I told myself as I prepared each dry sermon.

The initial awkwardness was replaced by grudging acceptance of each other, so long as I remained firmly in my place. As the Parish Priest was nearing eighty years old I learned to forgive his eccentricities.

The first silvery streaks were painted in the skyline as I wandered down the driveway from the Parochial House. Lost in the beauty of God's creation I began reading my matins, unaware of any other presence nearby.

The soft voice startled me and I instinctively stepped back. "There is nothing to fear Your Grace," spoke the lady in white.

'Lady in white' is such a poor description. She stood by the gateposts at the entrance to the driveway, bathed in a 'whiteness' that defies description. The fragile rays of the morning light seemed to envelop her, adding to the purity of the colour. Her clothing was almost biblical, the white robe falling from the shoulders to her feet. As I gazed transfixed the thought struck me that she could have been the Holy Virgin had she been dressed in blue. Eventually I was able to compose myself. "I'm afraid you have promoted me well beyond my abilities. Your Grace is reserved for Cardinals and Archbishops. I am a simple curate, so Father will suffice."

Her eyes seemed to look into my soul as I felt paralysed by her presence. Again she spoke, "you will be a Prince of the church. Within one month you will be the Parish Priest."

If I were to say that she simply faded away a listener would consider me mad. In modern parlance the beautiful lady of divine purity dematerialised. I rushed through my matins and ran to open the church. The canon found me there still praying at midday. "It's time you were off doing your rounds," he growled and returned to the Parochial House.

Each morning I looked for my white lady but she failed to materialise.

Exactly three weeks following my hallucination (for that is what I decided it was) my elderly superior earned his eternal rest. The internment service joyous, led by his Lordship the Bishop, attended by every parishioner for miles around. Everyone had a story to tell and his Lordship listened to all, with good grace. Afterwards in the Parochial House his Lordship informed me of my elevation to Parish Priest and his hope that I would move the parish into the twentieth century.

It took some time but eventually the parishioners accepted singing and music in the church and occasionally seeing their Parish Priest casually dressed. For two years I laboured to introduce mothers' clubs, sports clubs, art and drama in an attempt to make the church central to the lives of the parishioners. Some elderly folk drove five miles to attend Mass in the next village but gradually I wore them down with home visits, seeking their ideas and involving them in parish activities.

Life settled into a harmonious routine. I loved my parishioners and they loved me. I became convinced that these were the happiest days of my life.

I was wandering idly through the cemetery that lay outside the Parochial House when my 'white lady' reappeared. Yet, this time her gown was cream rather than white and I felt a little disappointment at the change. "It is time for change Your Grace," she murmured.

I asked what she meant. "You have served your time, now it is time to move on. Go to the house of James and welcome him back to the church."

"How can I do that?" I asked, "My predecessor excommunicated that man for sodomy."

"Do it" she murmured before disappearing.

I went to the church for guidance. Homosexuality was no longer considered to be satanic but still the church disapproved.

Next day I drove to James' mansion. He welcomed me with great grace, inviting me into his home. Over several hours we found we had much in common so I invited him to return to the church. I stressed that the church would never accept the act of homosexuality but the repentant sinner could be loved and forgiven.

James expressed his gratitude at my invitation but declined to attend services. Before I left he impressed upon me his joy and his hope that I would return. Not only did I return but my visits increased until he began to see me as part of his non-existent family.

I had been calling for more than six months when James rang one day to give me some bad news; he had cancer of the liver which had spread leaving him only a few weeks to live. I immediately drove to his home to offer my condolences. I found him in good spirits, insisting he was reconciled to his fate. He had one last favour to ask me if I would perform his funeral Mass and oversee his burial.

It would be wrong to say that I was happy to fulfil his dying wishes, as I now considered him to be a dear friend. I agreed to his request.

James died just five weeks later, with me in attendance. I had to administer the last rites and James died peacefully. I believed he was in the arms of God.

Following the internment James' solicitor invited me to the reading of the will. There were only two bequests; his money, house and estate would be left to the church, to be used as I considered fit. Personal items contained in the local vault were to be left to me personally.

I informed his Lordship who agreed that James' estates should be sold with the money being paid directly into the Diocesan Fund.

The sale raised ten million pounds for the church and his Lordship decided that I should be rewarded for my 'great work' (his words) for the church. One week later I was anointed as an Auxiliary Bishop, directly responsibly to his Lordship.

My life changed dramatically, not least in learning to accept being addressed as Your Lordship. At first I had attempted to explain that my superior was his Lordship the

Bishop, while I was the Auxiliary Bishop. Then I gave up trying and accepted the title.

Five years of frenetic fund raising, socialising promoting the church and endless coffee following confirmation and I am promoted to Bishop, receiving my purple hat from His Grace the Cardinal. At the celebrations afterwards His Grace joked that he would have to watch me. He was seventy two years old and in three years he must hand in his resignation to the Holy Father. The Holy Father did not have to accept the Cardinal's resignation but with a young thrusting Bishop like me in the wings one never knew!

When I suggest that at forty years old I had too much to learn to be considered for any further honours. Besides I had just been appointed as a bishop and might make a complete mess of it. Even as I said it the words sounded hollow and the wise old Cardinal's eyes told me that he knew it.

Three years is but a short time in the life of a bishop and I was not at all surprised when the Holy Father accepted the Cardinal's resignation and appointed another person as head of the Church in my country. I was only forty three, I had plenty of time. Not once did I reflect back on the happy days as a curate; I was the Lord Bishop and my time had come.

My opportunity came in the strangest way. The Holy Mother Church was beset with scandals and His Holiness sought out people he could trust: People who were unsullied, people who would speak out against injustice and people who would walk in the shoes of the victims.

I was not first choice to lead the investigations, nor the second or third. Primate after Primate either refused the poisoned chalice or were themselves tainted, until the Holy Father's eye fell on me.

I was summoned to Rome, thoroughly investigated and tested to the limits. Then my work began, removing the dead wood, prosecuting the perpetrators of abuse and defending the innocents.

For five years I never ceased, nowhere was too far to go, nothing too insignificant to investigate, no one above the law.

But the human spirit can only bear 'human efforts', the superhuman wears one down and I was only human. I was in my office in Rome when the pain struck, my chest on fire, my left arm useless and for the first time I believed I was dying. I did not die but spent several weeks in hospital in the Vatican recovering from a major heart attack.

The new Holy Father visited me in my hospital bed, blessed me and informed me that this stage of my work was finished. I began to protest, I was not yet fifty, too young to be retired.

The Holy Father smiled gently, "Not retired, re-employed in another capacity."

I thanked the Holy Father and committed the great faux pas of falling asleep in his presence.

I was received back in my own country with great pomp and splendour. The newspapers trumpeted the fact that, at forty eight years old I was the youngest Archbishop in the country's history.

I was received at the airport by the Prime Minister, Cabinet Ministers, Bishops, clergy and a large number of laity.

As we drove in convoy through the capital city I allowed myself a smile, the 'Head Boy' had done rather well after all!

I am back strolling in the cathedral grounds as dawn is breaking. I think how the habits of a lifetime carry on as I await the rise of the sun.

The voice comes out of nowhere; it is harsh, grating and bile filled, "You have done well, Prince of the Church." Suddenly she is beside me, dressed in black from head to toe. Her face is the personification of all that is vile and hateful. Again she speaks, "The old cardinal will soon be dead and you will be Cardinal Archbishop. What then Prince of the Church does the Holy See await?"

I confess that I have not given it a moment's thought. The old crone cackles, "No not a thought but many thoughts!" I am forced to admit to myself that the following in the footsteps of Saint Peter would have its merits.

The crone was speaking again, "What makes you think you deserve such an honour?"

"I have harmed no man," I said, "I have worked for the glorification of the Church and the enrichment of the poor."

The crone cackles, "Did you work for the enrichment of your old Parish Priest?" she demands.

"Of course I did," I reply hotly.

"Did you not walk away when you saw him stumble and unable to reach his tablets?"

"I went to the chapel, as I had planned." My response lacks conviction.

"And what of James' millions?" she demands.

"All given to the Diocese," I respond.

"Oh yes but what about the treasures in the bank's vault?" she is remorseless.

"What treasures?" I demand.

"The collection of gold coins, the bag of diamonds, the antique gold timepieces and the Francis Bacon portrait? What happened to them?"

Before I had a chance to reply she spat out her own answer, "A million for the gold pieces, another for the diamonds all deposited in your own bank account!"

Mercilessly she proceeds, "The timepieces placed in a safety deposit box, no doubt for their own safe keeping and what did you do with the Bacon?"

Please God, I think let this stop but there is no respite. "A Bacon painting would have brought in five million pounds think of the lives you might have saved in Africa."

I have no answer, the exquisitely beautiful painting has followed me throughout my travels. I am intoxicated by its sheer beauty, how could I possibly let it go?

"Bad and as all these things are, you have done much worse, haven't you Your Grace?"

I blanch under her malignant stare.

"What compassion did you show to your fellow churchmen, where was the love, the teachings of Christ when you acted as judge and executioner towards the accused?"

I can only splutter, "The Holy Father thought I did a good job."

"The Holy Father was not in the room when you advised your colleagues to take the old Roman way out of their problems. Who gave you the right to play God? Many might call you a mass murderer if they knew how you advised the accused to open a vein and spare the Church further embarrassment."

"I was thinking only of the Church, and the Holy Father exonerated me of all guilt!" I am shouting in the early morning air.

There is no end to it. "When more than fifty m‌‌ ‌‌ took their lives using the same ancient method ‌‌ ‌‌ ‌ly Father not question your ways?"

I can only assume he was g‌‌ ‌‌ ‌‌ ‌oblem reduced but I was not going to say that to h‌‌

Her stare is baleful, filled with hatre‌‌ ‌ut I take a firm grip on my Bible and challenge her. "Who are you?" I demand. "Are you the devil incarnate?"

"No," she replies, "Some say I do not exist, some call me your internal critic, some say conscience while others name me your super ego."

She fixed me with a stare that left me no doubt as to my destiny. "Most would say I am your eternal soul."